CW00406603

The Chocolatier's Cottage

De-ann Black

Published 2017

The Chocolatier's Cottage

ISBN: 9781521433515

Also by De-ann Black (Romance, Action/Thrillers & Children's books). See her Amazon Author page or website for further details about her books, screenplays, illustrations, art and fabric designs.

www.De-annBlack.com

Romance:

The Sewing Shop
Heather Park
The Tea Shop by the Sea
The Bookshop by the Seaside
The Sewing Bee
The Quilting Bee
Snow Bells Wedding
Snow Bells Christmas
Summer Sewing Bee
The Chocolatier's Cottage
Christmas Cake Chateau
The Beemaster's Cottage
The Sewing Bee By The Sea
The Flower Hunter's Cottage

The Christmas Knitting Bee
The Sewing Bee & Afternoon Tea
The Vintage Sewing & Knitting Bee
Shed In The City
The Bakery By The Seaside
Champagne Chic Lemonade Money
The Christmas Chocolatier
The Christmas Tea Shop & Bakery
The Vintage Tea Dress Shop In Summer
Oops! I'm The Paparazzi
The Bitch-Proof Suit

Action/Thrillers:

Love Him Forever.
Someone Worse.
Electric Shadows.

The Strife Of Riley.
Shadows Of Murder.

Children's books:

Faeriefied.
Secondhand Spooks.
Poison-Wynd.

Wormhole Wynd.
Science Fashion.
School For Aliens.

Colouring books:

Summer Garden. Spring Garden. Autumn Garden. Sea Dream. Festive Christmas. Christmas Garden. Flower Bee. Wild Garden. Faerie Garden Spring. Flower Hunter. Stargazer Space. Bee Garden.

Embroidery books:

Floral Nature Embroidery Designs
Scottish Garden Embroidery Designs

Contents

CHAPTER ONE

Vintage Quilts

Mhairi dived down behind the chocolatier's rose bushes. It was almost midnight. Did this man never sleep? She thought he'd gone to bed, but oh no, there he was up again.

As she hid in his garden, she could see his tall, lightly tanned, manly physique pacing about in his front lounge through the cottage window. The curtains were open and the lights on. He was half exposed, wearing only his silk pyjama bottoms, bare chest toned and honed as tempting as his chocolate confections. If you were attracted to that sort of man, which she wasn't. Definitely not. He may be rich, handsome, successful, living in one of the lovely cottages on the edge of the seashore, but she'd never seen him smile. Not even when Thimble the dressmaker's cat entwined itself affectionately around his legs recently. The cat liked him, so that was a good sign, however, he hadn't paused to pet it. The fact that he was carrying a gorgeous three–tier chocolate cake wasn't an excuse.

Sharpen up, Mhairi, she scolded herself. Focus on stealth moves, keep low below the rose bushes to avoid being seen by the chocolatier. She swept strands of her sun–lightened, caramel–coloured hair back from her face and tightened her ponytail. She also tried not to snag her jumper on the thorns. It had taken her a month to knit it in a fine cotton yarn. She should've worn an old sweatshirt for her midnight raid on his dustbin, but she'd never raided anyone's bin before so she put her unprepared attire down to inexperience. She had no experience of sneaking around in the shadows, waiting to grab the beautiful vintage quilt he'd heartlessly thrown away as if it was rubbish. Who did that anyway? What prat threw a perfectly sewn vintage heirloom out with the cake debris? Obviously he did.

She wondered if by staring at him he sensed her watching him because he suddenly looked out the window.

She lay face down on the lawn, not daring to move. She waited a couple of minutes, which when you're nostril deep in blades of freshly mown grass, can seem like ages. But she was determined not to be beaten. She'd been stalking him since ten o'clock at night,

1

waiting for the chance to run round to his back garden, grab the unwanted quilt and then scarper to her own cottage further along the coast near the little shops at the harbour. He'd never know.

Hurry up and go to bed, she willed him. He was up at the crack of dawn most mornings melting his chocolate along with many of the local ladies' hearts. Sexy dark hair and a handsome face with deep blue eyes weren't his only assets. He liked to go for an early morning swim in the sea wearing tight trunks and nothing else. He didn't even drape a towel around his dripping wet body when he'd finished swimming a stretch of the shoreline. He'd emerge from the sea, glistening wet, looking like an athlete.

Luckily she was an early riser herself and her cottage had a view of the sea, so admiring him in the mornings required no effort whatsoever. Her quilting table and sewing machine were set up at the window. She couldn't help but gaze out at the sea. If the master chocolatier was part of the view, it wasn't her fault he'd become a daily distraction. And she wasn't the only one. Ethel, Hilda and other ladies had commented about him during their weekly meetings at the local sewing bee. Two other good looking men who lived nearby enjoyed a morning swim, but it was the chocolatier who attracted Mhairi's interest.

The chocolatier had kept himself to himself since he'd arrived in the late spring. Even Ethel who spun and dyed her own yarn in her cottage didn't have much gossip on him, and Ethel knew everybody's business.

When Mhairi asked Ethel about the mysterious chocolatier, there wasn't a lot to tell.

'His name is Cuan McVey. He's a master chocolatier, in his early thirties, around the same age as you, Mhairi. He moved into the cottage in the late spring. He bought it from the previous owner, Jaec Midwinter, a chocolatier who rarely used it. The kitchen was specially kitted–out with all the necessary equipment for making chocolate creations, but the previous chocolatier worked in the city and found no time or use for the cottage so he sold it to Cuan. Since he moved in, he's been very private, except when he displays his hot–bod during his daily dip in the sea.'

One of the local flower growers had been hired to keep the cottage's beautiful rose garden trimmed and cared for. Roses grew around the front door. Rambling roses were entwined on the trellis archway at the side of the cottage leading on to the back garden where more roses and a wonderful selection of flowers created an old–fashioned garden that suited the traditional style of the cream–painted cottage. The side walls had a profusion of pink roses climbing up them, making the cottage one of the most romantic–looking along the coastline.

Rose hedges provided a fragrant and blossom–filled border around the property. Even though it was by the sea, the soil was rich. Mhairi had never seen the cottage in winter, but in the summer it reminded her of the vintage rose print quilts she loved to sew — with colours ranging from palest pink blossom to dusky rose and dark green leaves. Yes, it really was one of the prettiest cottages around. The flower hunter owned a heritage cottage nearby filled with plants from around the world, and was the most beautiful garden she'd ever seen, but when it came to romanticism, the chocolatier's cottage was hard to beat.

Cottages were dotted along the shore and up towards the tree filed inland where some had a high–top view of the spectacular bay, sparkling sea and islands far off in the distance. The dressmaker's cottage was hidden deep within the trees, while other cottages such as the one Mhairi was living in were set right on the cusp of the shore.

She'd moved from the city to house–sit her aunt's crafting cottage. Her aunt was a professional quilter and was abroad in America attending several quilting and craft fairs, exhibitions and events throughout the summer. She'd asked her niece to look after the cottage, which was a perfect working holiday for Mhairi, herself a quilter.

Mhairi had been wanting to get away from the city, from the pressures of flat–sharing and trying to set up a shop but unable to afford a lease. City shop leases were too expensive.

The cottage by the sea in the Scottish Highlands, where she'd often enjoyed a holiday, was ideal. She was free to work on her new quilt block designs, sew quilts galore, relax in the lovely little cottage with its pretty garden, and pretend she never had to leave and go back to the city when her aunt came home. That wasn't until the end of August. This was mid June. She had the whole summer to live in one of the most beautiful parts of Scotland without a care in the world — except how to save the quilt that Cuan had cast aside.

3

She knew what it was to be cast aside, unwanted and of no further use. When it came to romance, her choice of boyfriends was *rotten*. No other word described it better. Rotten choices. Rotten swines. All three of them in five years. So stuff relationships and romance. She was set for a summer of fun, including ogling the chocolatier even though he never smiled.

If he'd shown a smidgen of humour or stopped to talk to people in the post office that doubled as a grocery shop, or showed some element of not being grumpy, she'd have chapped his door and asked him if she could take the quilt instead of lurking in the shadows, waiting until he was asleep before she pounced on it.

She took a deep breath. An abundance of blooms filled the air with a heady night–time scent. It reminded her of tea roses and gardenia.

Finally, the lights went out inside his cottage.

Mhairi got ready to tackle the assault course through to his back garden via the rose trellis. She climbed up the trellis to clamber over the high gate, jumped down and scurried to his bin area. And there it was — the quilt she'd seen, folded on top of a box beside the dustbin. She'd seen it earlier that afternoon when walking along the pathway behind his cottage. She hadn't been spying on him. She'd spotted it while meandering by. Some people were good at spotting butterflies or birds. She was a quilter, and recognised the quality of what was being thrown away.

In the Scottish Highlands the summer evening light rarely faded to darkness. It simply dimmed before turning up again to full brightness in the morning. In the twilight glow Mhairi saw the beautiful quilt, and as she lifted it, she found two other equally lovely quilts underneath it.

He'd thrown out three vintage quilts? How dare he! She had a mind to chap his door and tell him what she thought of him, but she decided to cut and run with the quilts while she had a chance.

Now laden with three large quilts, climbing back over the gate via the trellis would be difficult. She opted to scramble over the hedge at its lowest point, noticing a dip in it near a rose tree.

That was her mistake.

As she walked across the lawn her movement set off the security system consisting of a spotlight that dazzled her startled face while a hidden camera snapped her picture.

Blinking to gain her senses, unaware she'd been photographed, she scrambled over the hedge and made a run for it.

'Who's there?' she heard the chocolatier shout.

Keep running, keep going. Jeez these quilts were heavy and awkward, but not as awkward as having to explain to Mr Grumpy what she'd done.

As she bolted for home, she glanced back at the chocolatier's cottage. Every light in the house was on, casting a glow on to his garden. And there was Cuan, still clad in his silky pyjama bottoms, standing out front looking for the culprit.

Mhairi put a spurt on, darted into her cottage, kept the lights off and gasped for breath. She dumped the quilts on the hall table and peered out through the letterbox. Yes, there he was, pacing the esplanade like a predatory wolf, scanning the area for the intruder.

Her heart lurched when he stopped and looked over at her cottage. Again, was it that sense of being watched? She shut the letterbox and didn't move, hardly breathed, in case he saw her shadow through the tiny panes of glass on the upper part of the door.

She waited until she thought he had to have gone, before crawling on all fours through to the lounge and peering out the window. He was walking back to his cottage. She couldn't see any further as he lived at the far end of the main shoreline. But she could sense his anger. Oh yes, she was glad he had no idea who she was.

Keeping the lights dimmed, she made a cup of tea to settle her nerves, still feeling slightly rattled by the unexpected security spotlight.

No one locked their doors around here. Keys were rusted into locks and never used. She hadn't anticipated he'd have a security system. Thankfully, she was certain he hadn't actually seen her. She was over the hedge and gone before he ran out of the cottage.

In the early morning light, Mhairi looked at the quilts. They were vintage all right. Worth quite a bit if she wanted to sell them, which she didn't. She planned to add them to her stash of traditional quilts. Then she reconsidered. No, she'd leave them here in her aunt's cottage.

When she studied the quilts she noticed that two of them were made from other quilts and probably baby blankets and items of clothing — made from memories of personal value. It seemed wrong to take the quilts away from where they belonged. Seashell, sail boats and seahorse motifs were part of the designs, as were sea thistles and little cottages, indicating they were sewn here in the local community.

Often it was hard to tell when a vintage quilt was sewn because it may have been part of an original quilt sewn in the past, but updated by others contributing their own little pieces to it, or replacing old and worn blocks, until it was difficult to know when one part began and another joined it. That was the beauty of quilting.

She looked carefully at the stitching. Expertly done. The colours were faded, but in their muted tones they'd become even more beautiful.

The bindings were so well done. Mhairi checked them closely. Not one part was loose or frayed. No repairs required. These quilts were sewn to last, and they had, and she was extra glad she'd risked the ire of the chocolatier to rescue them.

She shook them, ensuring no crumbs or grass were on them. They were clean, well cared for, and so she folded them and sat them on a shelf inside a cupboard with her aunt's other vintage quilts.

Sunlight shone through the window, pouring a liquid gold glow into the lounge. Mhairi opened the window and relished the summery sea air. She loved the start of the day, planning what she'd sew. She was working on a few projects, including traditional quilts. Perhaps she'd add pink seashells to one quilt and turquoise seahorses to the other. . .

The colours of the sea had inspired her to use fabrics in every shade from sea foam to aquamarine. She pictured one quilt she was sewing would be suitable for framing as wall art — a seascape. She'd stitched rows of waves, starfish, seaweed fronds and pieces of blue, green and amber coloured fabrics cut and sewn together like sea glass.

She raked through a pile of fabrics in her stash. Somewhere in there was a seahorse print material. The fabrics were separated by colour and she rummaged through the turquoise blues and. . . yes, she knew it was there. She pulled out the fat quarter of material and put it on her work table. If she fussy cut around the seahorses she could then sew them on to the quilt. And there were mermaids too!

She was set to start work when her tummy rumbled, reminding her she hadn't eaten breakfast. It had been an unsettled night.

6

She went through to the kitchen and checked the fridge. She'd run out of fresh milk to make breakfast, so she slipped into a little cotton dress and sandals, brushed her shoulder–length hair smooth and silky, added a slick of lippy and popped down to the post office for supplies.

A warm breeze blew through the fabric of her dress, emphasising her slender figure. Sometimes she was so busy sewing she forgot to eat. She'd always loved quilting, crafting and making things. Crochet was another hobby, and Ethel's new hand spun yarns were a joy to use for both crochet and knitting patterns.

A sea haze wafted over the sparkling turquoise water. Boats bobbed in the harbour, and the grocery shop beside the post office advertised their delicious ice cream.

The majority of people who lived in the little cottage community worked from home and made a living from all sorts of crafts including quilting, knitting, crocheting, sewing, sugarcraft, jewellery making and art. There was even an online craft magazine that had become very popular and had helped increase trade so much it was worthwhile for a city courier service to make at least three trips a week to pick up and deliver loads of parcels. The post office at the harbour thrived.

Thimble the black cat sat on the harbour wall watching her. This was strange, she thought. The cat didn't like being so near the water. He preferred to prowl the gardens and stay away from the harbour's edge. But it was definitely him. A tiny silver thimble dangled from his collar. She blinked and he'd gone. Scarpered probably when he heard the waves lapping gently on the shore.

Mhairi went into the post office for milk, morning rolls and a bottle of lemonade.

The postmaster knew her, but instead of giving her the usual cheery welcome he stared at her as if. . . she wasn't sure.

Ethel came in and smiled at her. 'Morning, Mhairi.' Ethel's silvery blonde hair was pinned up in a tidy bun, and a knitted lavender shawl was draped around her shoulders. Lavender and sea blue were her latest shades of yarn. Ethel often created her yarn colours to reflect the seasons. She was the only one in the locale with a pale blue painted cottage. She lived alone and ran her yarn business from home. 'We're in for another scorcher. What are you up to today?'

7

The postmaster interrupted. 'It's what she was up to last night that's the trouble.'

Mhairi and Ethel frowned. What was he talking about? And then he pointed to an A4 sheet of paper pinned up on the post office notice board where people could pay to advertise things wanted or for sale.

Mhairi's eyes widened when she saw what was pinned up — a wanted poster featuring her picture, looking like a demented squirrel caught in the glaring beam of the security light, clutching vintage quilts.

Ethel adjusted her spectacles. Was she seeing right?

'It is you, Mhairi, isn't it?' the postmaster said tentatively. He was sweet on Ethel and didn't want to upset either of them. But the poster didn't lie. It was her. A weird version of her, but definitely no doubt about who had taken the chocolatier's quilts. *Stolen* was the word highlighted.

Reward given to anyone with information on this woman who has STOLEN quilts from my garden at night.

'A reward?' gasped Ethel. 'The chocolatier's paying to have you hunted down? What were you up to, Mhairi? And are those vintage quilts you're clutching?'

Mhairi's world flipped. 'I can explain. . .'

'I'd love to hear your explanation,' a man's classy Scottish voice said. Cuan had entered the shop, but they'd been so focussed on the poster none of them had heard him.

Mhairi turned to face him. Jeez he was handsome, and clearly angry with her.

The three of them waited for what seemed an age for her to explain, but was probably only a few seconds. And unless she was mistaken, she saw him glance at the wanted poster and compare the demented squirrel to the lovely young woman standing in front of him.

'I was saving the quilts,' Mhairi managed to say.

'Saving them from what?' Ethel asked her, totally bewildered.

'From being thrown away. He'd flung them out with the rubbish. They were lying beside his bin.'

'Maybe he was airing them?' the postmaster suggested.

Mhairi's heart lurched. This hadn't occurred to her. She dared to look at the chocolatier. Thankfully, he didn't use this as an excuse.

8

He stepped closer, causing her heart to lurch again, but in a different way. He was standing too close to her, wearing a white shirt with the top buttons undone, exposing a hint of that honed chest of his. She had a flashback of him half naked in his cottage, then another of him glistening wet, emerging from the sea. A blush burned across her cheeks.

'You should look embarrassed,' the chocolatier scolded her, mistaking her hot blush for blame.

'You had no right to throw away those beautiful quilts,' she snapped at him.

He stepped even closer and looked down at her. She barely reached his shoulders in height. 'You had no right to steal them.'

Mhairi straightened and tried not to feel intimidated by his handsomeness or height. 'I wouldn't say I *stole* them,' she argued.

Cuan's gorgeous blue eyes skewered her. 'No, what word would you use?'

She thought for a moment and couldn't think of a pleasant alternative.

'Purloined,' the postmaster suggested.

'Yes,' Mhairi agreed, 'purloined.'

'They mean the same thing,' said Cuan.

'Not quite.' Purloined definitely sounded less thief–like.

The chocolatier gave her a sneery look.

'You can sneer all you want,' Mhairi told him, 'but what you did was wrong.'

'Oh and what you did was okay?'

'Someone had to save those quilts. You'd flung them out with your manky cake boxes.'

She swore she saw his nostrils flare. 'My cake boxes are expertly designed to house my artisan confections.' The indignation in his tone didn't miss her.

Mhairi stepped into his personal space and faced up at him. 'Listen, Mr hoity–toity. You were casting aside heritage quilts. Some things are just not done. That was one of them. Those quilts are valuable and have been cared for and protected for decades. You can't just throw them out with your sticky cake boxes.'

He started to lecture her on the finer points of his artisan cakes and confectionery, but Mhairi had listened enough.

9

'Get a grip,' she shouted at him. 'They're just ruddy chocolate cakes.'

That comment tipped the balance.

'They're not just chocolate cakes. They are artisan creations.'

'They're made to eat. People munch them. My quilts are carefully crafted. Some are pieces of art.'

'Art quilts?'

'You can scoff, but yes, art quilts. Many types of quilts are framed and hung as art, but you'd know or appreciate this if you looked further than that chocolate–dominated nose of yours.'

He sneered.

'Continue sneering, but my quilts will outlast your cakes. Some may even become vintage one day. I hope that no one will throw them out with the cake crumbs.'

'You said the quilts are valuable.'

'Yes, they are.'

'So you're planning to sell them and make money from them?' The accusation in his voice irritated her, but at least he didn't seem to be asking her to give them back.

'No, I'm not.'

He clearly didn't believe her. Those sexy blue eyes showed the depth of his disbelief. 'What are you going to do with them?'

'Keep them safe with other vintage quilts. Preserve and protect them from damage.'

He looked uncertain. 'You're not planning to make a profit from them?'

'Of course not.'

'You still stole them, without asking me.'

'If you'd shown any sense of pleasantness, instead of wearing a permanent scowl, I would have asked you.'

'You didn't ask me because. . . '

'You're perpetually grumpy.'

He took the verbal slap on the jaw, and tried to appear indignant, but she'd stung him.

She followed through with another remark. 'And too taken with yourself and your fancy pants chocolate cakes.'

The insult cut deep. A challenge brewed in the depths of his eyes. 'You think you could bake something like that?'

'Well, yes, maybe, sort of, definitely.'

'Okay then. This time tomorrow. Bring the best chocolate cake you can bake here to the post office.'

'You're challenging me to a choccie cake bake?'

'Yes, unless you're sprouting chicken tail feathers.'

'Okay. And taste matters, not just fancy swirly chocolate decorations.'

'Agreed.'

'Is she allowed to have anyone help her?' Ethel asked.

'She can have all the help she wants.' He sounded so confident, as if it didn't matter if she had help from Ethel and other ladies.

Mhairi nodded firmly. The challenge was set.

'Remember,' he said, 'this time tomorrow morning.' He went to stomp away.

Mhairi tore the wanted poster down and thrust it at him. 'You can take this with you and stick it somewhere else.'

He scrunched it into a ball, tightening his fist around it.

She watched him stride off.

'Did I just accept a challenge from Cuan McVey?' she said.

Ethel nodded. 'Can you bake, Mhairi?'

'I can rustle up a strawberry and cream sponge. I bake my own Christmas cakes.' Then she remembered. 'My aunt has an old–fashioned recipe book. There's a great recipe for chocolate cake in it. It tastes delicious. Layers of chocolate sponge with chocolate buttercream and ganache icing.'

'What's ganache?' asked the postmaster.

'Smooth, silky icing made with melted chocolate and cream that you pour over the cake like a glaze.'

'It sounds tasty,' he said.

Mhairi nodded. 'Totally scrumptious. Since we can't beat him on fancy pants presentation, we'll tackle him on taste.'

The postmaster pointed to the fridge. 'Fresh cartons of cream were delivered this morning with the milk.'

'Ideal,' said Mhairi.

CHAPTER TWO

Old–Fashioned Chocolate Cake

Mhairi hurried back to her cottage. It was a working house, with tables where quilts were pieced together like a fabric jigsaw puzzle, and a longarm quilting machine. A thread rack could give a city's haberdashery a run for its money in the selection of threads, of various weights, depending on the use.

The lounge was the hub of the two–bedroom cottage, and reminded Mhairi of a crafter's paradise rather than a living room. Everything that could be quilted was quilted, from the sofa coverings and cushions to the sewing machine cover and tablemats. Even the cotton material of the curtains had a pretty patchwork quilt print.

The piles of fabric pieces, finished quilts and items being made, sprawled from the lounge into one of the bedrooms, which was used as a storeroom. Mhairi slept in the other bedroom at the back of the cottage, her aunt's room, the only one with a bed. When Mhairi came to stay for a holiday, she slept on a folding camp bed or on the sofa. There were no shortages of quilts to keep her warm.

The cottage had a homely feel to it even though it was like living in a quilt–maker's dream shop. Mhairi loved it, and couldn't imagine anywhere else she'd rather be during the summer.

She rummaged through the dresser drawers and found the recipe book. She flicked through the index hoping she'd remembered the name of the cake. Yes, there it was. An old–fashioned recipe for chocolate cake. Her aunt used to make it and it was delicious. Sometimes the old methods were the best. She scribbled down the list of ingredients, some of which were in the kitchen cupboard, others she'd buy from the grocery shop or borrow from Ethel.

Ethel phoned her. 'I've alerted the ladies of the bee, and a couple of them are expert bakers. They're happy to help.'

'My aunt has a great recipe and the kitchen's well enough equipped. The oven is good, so if anyone wants to drop by, I'm going to get started.'

Mhairi rattled off the ingredients needed, including sugar paste to make edible flower decorations for the top of the cake. 'I'm going to make sugarcraft roses.'

'I'll organise the sugar paste, flour and butter. And chocolate. We'll need loads of chocolate and cocoa powder.'

And so their plan of action was set.

Within an hour, several women were bustling around Mhairi's cottage, getting everything ready.

'This is the biggest cake tin I've got,' Mhairi said, unsure if it was big enough.

Judith, the dressmaker's assistant, turned up. The cottage door was open, letting in the warm breeze. Judith, a small, sturdy woman in her fifties with blonde hair, walked in carrying two bags. She smiled at Mhairi.

'The dressmaker heard about your challenge, and sent me to bring you this. It's the largest cake tin we have. Catering size. She thought it would be useful.'

Mhairi grabbed it. 'Thank you, this is brilliant.' She paused. 'How did the dressmaker know about this?'

Judith simply smiled. 'She knows everything that goes on.' She pointed to a small bag inside the cake tin. 'There are several fondant tea roses as well. Handy for decorating the cake.'

It was said that the dressmaker was fey and sewed magic into the dresses she made. She was wealthy and often contributed financially to the local community. Her dresses were bought and worn by film stars and celebrities. It was also said that Thimble was a fey cat, sent to watch and listen to the goings on in the local community, and to relay this to the dressmaker. Whether true or fanciful, Mhairi was delighted to have the dressmaker's involvement.

Judith stayed to help with the baking. Flour, cocoa powder, butter, eggs, sugar, cream and icing galore went into the cake creation.

They started at lunchtime and by five o'clock they'd finished. The cake had little chocolate leaves and pink sugar roses added to the top as decoration. Mhairi used the rose templates from her quilt blocks to design and fashion the flowers from sugar paste. These were indeed a work of art. She also added the fondant tea roses.

Ethel stood back to admire their handiwork. 'Classic.'

Judith smiled. 'It smells delicious.'

It did. Ganache, smooth as liquid silk, had been poured over the cake as the perfect icing. When ready, the sugar and fondant roses were added, and then the cake was placed on a silver foil cake board.

Before she left, Judith handed the other bag to Mhairi. 'The dressmaker also wanted you to have this.' She gave her a beautiful tea dress. 'It should fit, being a wraparound. She said you'd know when to wear this dress.'

It was made from vintage rose and cream printed fabric, stitched by the dressmaker herself.

'Thank you. This is perfect.' Mhairi held the dress up and admired it in the mirror.

'I'll tell the dressmaker you're happy with it,' said Judith.

As the women filtered out of the cottage, Mhairi caught a glimpse of Cuan walking along the esplanade. He glanced over. Had he been baking for hours or did he already have a cake he'd use to beat her at the challenge?

She breathed in the warm early evening air. It didn't matter. The cake they'd baked was up to the challenge, though her heart was in jeopardy if she was to resist the temptation of the handsome chocolatier.

Mhairi went for a walk along the esplanade in the late evening light. She'd worked on her quilting projects, trying out new designs for blocks and motifs. But she couldn't settle for thinking about the confrontation in the morning with Cuan.

She continued along the esplanade. The silvery sea was smooth and calm, unlike her. She felt ruffled and edgy.

A solitary light shone from the chocolatier's cottage. Was he in there working on a masterpiece to flatten her baking efforts? Or was he busy getting on with his business?

She didn't walk any closer, and turned around to head back home and get some sleep. The last man she expected to see walking towards her was Cuan. One of the little shops opened late some nights. Perhaps he'd popped down there, though she got the impression he'd walked past her cottage as that was the direction he'd come from.

What should she do? Walk past, glaring daggers at him? Pretend not to notice him? Though as they were the only two people on the esplanade she could hardly miss him.

Had he been spying on her cottage? She'd left a lamp on, having planned to be out for a short walk. Wouldn't it be weird, she thought, if they'd both been spying on each other.

'Finished baking?' he said, approaching her.

'Yes. Have you?'

He nodded.

They were still walking towards each other. She planned to keep walking. She didn't want to stop and chat to her rival, but he had other ideas and made a point of stopping right in front of her, making it awkward for her to simply walk past.

'I've been thinking things over,' he said, 'and you can keep the quilts if you want them.'

'I do. I've stored them with other vintage quilts.' And he wasn't getting them back without a fight.

'I'm glad they've found a good home.'

She didn't know if he was being trite, truthful or tricky. It was hard to read his body language when all six foot plus of him was standing there on a hot night making her wish there was a cold sea breeze. Her little cotton dress should've kept her temperature under control, but it didn't.

He'd changed his white shirt and now wore a dark blue one, sexily unbuttoned. The warm night merited wearing something cool, but the effect it had on her was the complete opposite. In the quietude she wondered if he could hear her heart pounding. He had a potent effect on her, damn him! She only had to look at him to feel. . . well. . . flustered and flushed.

'It's your own fault,' he said.

She blinked out of her thoughts.

'If you hadn't been so stubborn, I'd never have challenged you.'

Mhairi gasped. The cheek of him!

'So it's my fault you threw away the quilts, and my fault you suggested I bake a chocolate cake that's better than yours?'

'You caused the situation by sneaking around in my rose bushes.'

'I've already explained to you that I thought you were unapproachable.'

'And grumpy. Perpetually grumpy I think you said.'

Mhairi shrugged. 'Well, you are. I've never seen you smile.'

'I have a lot on my mind.'

'And that prevents you from smiling?'

'Maybe I don't feel like smiling.'

'No, you prefer to sneer.'

He sneered.

She pointed at him. 'Exactly.'

'Do you want to call off the challenge?' he offered.

'The sensible part of me says, yes, because it's a silly challenge. You're a master chocolatier. I have no chance against your expertise. But the stubborn part of me says, no way, especially as I spent hours baking the best chocolate cake I've ever made. With help from Ethel and other ladies.'

'Perhaps you've baked a winner after all?' There was a hint of admiration in his tone.

Mhairi looked up at him and spoke in a level manner. 'We both know how this will go tomorrow. You'll win by a country mile. Even though my cake is delicious, I can't compete with the levels of flavoursome expertise you've acquired over the years working as a chocolatier.'

A flicker of sadness or perhaps guilt crossed his handsome features.

'Then we'll argue. I'll continue to be stubborn and probably insult you horribly. You'll stomp off and everyone left standing in the post office after the rumpus will scoff the cakes.'

'And we'll all live stubbornly ever after,' he said.

'The closest to a happy ending we can hope for.' She stepped past him. 'I'd better go. I've still to assemble a cake box before getting some sleep.' She started to walk away.

'Try not to insult me too horribly,' he called after her.

'I will, if you try to smile.'

She kept walking. Did he smile a little at her comment she wondered? Probably not.

'I can give you a cake box,' he shouted.

She stopped and turned. His cottage was right there. He could run in and fetch one while she waited near his rose bushes.

'Come in for a moment,' he beckoned her. 'I'll give you a box. Then you can jump straight into bed.'

She gawped at him.

'What I meant was. . . you can go straight into your own bed. . . without having to make a cake box.'

She smiled to herself, enjoying him flounder.

He walked up the garden path and she followed him. He unlocked his front door and went inside. 'Step in for a minute.'

She did. She left the door open and the heady fragrance of roses accompanied her in.

The aroma of chocolate wafted through the cottage, mingling with the scent of the flowers.

She looked around while he hurried into the kitchen at the back. She peeked in the two front rooms — the lounge and front bedroom were elegantly decorated in cream and neutral shades. Unlike her cottage, Cuan slept in this bedroom and there was no evidence of his work spilling into it.

She wandered through to the back bedroom that was like an extension of the kitchen, with tables laden with cakes and boxes of luxury chocolates. This was the hub of Cuan's world where product development and new recipes were created. Notebooks filled with secret recipes and techniques lay open on one of the tables. One book listed various flavours to add to the ingredients. She skimmed part of the list — lime, orange, raspberry, mint, whisky, champagne, tea and rose syrup.

A laptop was set up on a desk near the window with a view of the garden. A light was on in the summerhouse. The doors were wide open revealing two garden chairs in need of cushions. She'd always wanted a summerhouse where she could relax on sunny days, shelter from thunder storms, listen to the rain while breathing in the scents of the flowers, and snuggle cosy in wintertime.

The two–bedroom cottage was quite spacious, similar in design to Ethel's, built around the same time. They were two of the oldest houses with extra large back gardens. Ethel had an extension added on to hers and it allowed her to expand her yarn business. During Mhairi's brief excursion into Cuan's back garden, she hadn't taken in the extent of the potential it had to add another room for his chocolatier work.

She walked through the arched doorway to the large kitchen which was kitted–out like a hotel kitchen — clean, efficient, top of the range cooking equipment, fridge, freezer and cooling storage. There was also a separate kitchenette area in the far corner with its own cooker, fridge and sink for personal use.

Cuan selected cake boxes for her. 'A catering courier picks up my deliveries every few days. I know the kitchen looks packed, but he's due for a pick–up in the morning.'

A magnificent chocolate cake sat in pride of place, and it appeared that he'd been putting the finishing touches of fine carved chocolate hearts on to each of the four–tiers. Was this the cake she was up against?

Cuan saw her staring at it. 'Don't worry, I'm not taking that to the post office tomorrow.'

She smiled. 'You'd have needed a forklift to carry it.'

'It's for an exclusive wedding. Not mine,' he added firmly. 'I've never been married, and have no plans to do so.'

Her heart sank, though why should she care that Cuan wasn't the marrying kind? He saw her disappointment.

'What I mean is, I'm not involved with anyone, but if I was dating someone I really liked then marriage would be a consideration. And you?'

'Unmarried and not looking for romance. Given up on it.'

'Bad relationships to blame for your reluctance to romance?'

'Rotten relationships.'

'That's at least something we have in common. I've never managed to pick the right woman.'

He handed her two folded cardboard cake boxes.

'Here are two boxes, different sizes, standard and large. One should fit your cake, unless you've baked a two–tier, and if so, you'll need both boxes.'

She looked at them. It should be easy enough to fold them.

'I'll assemble them for you. Being a crafter you should be handy at things like this, but it'll save you time.'

He folded them quickly. She watched his elegant fingers smooth every crease. Each small gesture from this man set her senses aflame.

She lifted the boxes up and carried them out.

'I'll carry them for you,' he said.

'They're light, I can manage.'

'I'll walk back with you to your cottage.'

'There's really no need. It's quite safe here. No one I know, except you, even locks their doors at night.'

18

'I insist. Besides, I dropped a note through your letterbox earlier. That's where I'd been. I thought you'd be asleep and wrote the note, but when I got near the cottage I saw a light on. I knocked, but you were out. I put the note through and headed back here and that's when I saw you walking along the esplanade.'

'I'll read the note when I get back. There's absolutely no need to bother.'

'No, don't read it. It's unnecessary now that we've chatted. I was offering to cancel the challenge. So don't waste time reading it.'

She got the impression he might have said something he now regretted.

Cuan would not be shaken off, and as they walked back to her cottage she asked about his work.

'What made you want to become a chocolatier?'

'My father was a patissier and my mother was a baker. I started out in the same line of work as my father, then specialised as a chocolatier. They now live down south. They have their own shops and do very well.' He glanced over at her. 'What about you?'

'I've been sewing and crafting for as long as I can remember. My mother and my teachers encouraged me. It seemed the natural profession to work in. I think it helps when you love your work. Quilting is especially fascinating. There's always another new fabric, design or thread to use. I hoard scraps of fabric like a collector. I never tire of quilting. I also worked in advertising to make ends meet when first starting out.' She paused and sounded melancholy. 'We lost dad a long time ago. Mum lives in Canada now with her second husband. She's happy. We keep in touch, perhaps not as often as we should, but she has her own life and I'm truly happy for her.'

They reached her cottage and she opened the door.

She caught the look on his face that it had been unlocked, confirming what she'd said about him locking his cottage.

A cream–coloured envelope lay on the polished wood floor. She lifted it up but he grabbed it off her.

'Give me the letter, Cuan.'

He held it out of her reach. 'You really don't need it.'

'I really do, now hand it over.'

She made a determined grab for it, but he used his height against her, raising it up out of her reach. He stepped outside, giving her a

19

momentary advantage as she stood two steps up and if she jumped up just a little bit she could grab it.

Cuan hadn't expected her to leap at him, and stumbled back, trying to evade Mhairi and avoid stamping on her garden flowers — an assortment of blooms, though partially closed for the night.

As Cuan stumbled, Mhairi overreached and tumbled with him. He landed on his back on a patch of lawn amid the pansies and peonies. The soft grass broke his fall, and being a fit fellow, he was unhurt. Mhairi was lucky too. She landed on Cuan.

She felt the muscles of his chest and toned abdominals beneath the fabric of her dress.

They were face to face, and it looked like she had him pinned down.

'Give me the letter,' she insisted, still trying to take it off him.

She almost managed it, but the sound of someone nearby made them both pause.

Mhairi peered through the flowers. 'It's the owner of the grocery shop. He was probably open late tonight. He's locking up and looking over here,' she whispered. 'Don't move until he's gone. I don't want anyone seeing us like this. It looks bad, if you know what I mean.'

He nodded. He knew exactly what she meant.

He kept his voice low and she felt his breath brush across her cheeks as he said, 'How long will we have to lie here like this?'

'Oh, about an hour or so,' she whispered.

She saw the whites of his eyes and felt his stomach tense beneath her, which caused all sorts of reactions within her.

'Relax, Cuan. I was winding you up. He'll be gone in a minute.'

Cuan's chest puffed up when he realised. 'Why you little. . .' He put one hand lightly on her throat and pretended to throttle her, causing her to laugh.

'Ssh!' he scolded her. 'We'll never be able to explain this away. Rolling around in your bushes late at night. The gossipmongers around here will turn our reputations to toast.'

She couldn't stop laughing, and the panicky look on his face make her laugh even louder.

Cuan grabbed her, rolled on top of her, reversing their positions, and pinioned her to the lawn. 'Quiet!'

She snickered.

He held her down, and she loved every moment of it. Shame on her, but what the heck.

'Behave yourself. You're a bad influence on me. Last night you were hiding in the bushes at my cottage, now you've got me rolling about in your bushes, in a compromising position.'

'Don't worry, you haven't compromised me.'

Sexy blue eyes looked down at her and his lips were a breath away as he said, 'Believe me, I'm trying not to, but you're a damned temptation, Mhairi.'

That was the first time he'd said her name, and something in his tone, the way he pronounced her name right — Vaa–ree, sent tingles through her. What a sexy beast he was.

The grocer drove off in his van.

'Sounds like he's gone now,' she said.

Cuan paused and peeked over the plants. 'He has.'

And yet he was still lying on top of her. Not that she was complaining. There were worse ways to spend an evening than pinned down in the garden by a luscious chocolatier.

He stood up, held out his hand and helped her up.

She managed to grab the letter with her other hand, keeping it hidden. He seemed to have momentarily forgotten about it.

She brushed bits of flowers and leaves from her dress and went into the cottage.

'You've got grass stains on your—' he indicated her backside.

She pulled the skirt of the dress around. 'On my bahookie.'

And that's when he noticed the letter in her hand.

'Why you cheeky monkey,' he said, and tried to grab it off her.

She stuffed it down the front of her dress. 'The letter is mine.'

Cuan stepped close to her and said in a seductive tone, 'If I was less of a gentleman, I'd retrieve it right now.'

Her stomach filled with butterflies at the thought of this. She smiled up at him. 'Thank goodness you'll behave yourself.' And then she laughed.

'You can laugh, Mhairi, but let me tell you, you're a bundle of trouble.'

'I've been told that I am untameable.' Rotten boyfriends had mentioned this, more than once.

21

'After tomorrow's cake contest, I may make that our next challenge,' he said, 'but it could take me all summer to tame a wildcard like you.' He started to walk away.

'By then it'll be too late,' she said with a note of triumph.

He looked back. 'Why is that? You live here, don't you?'

'Only for the summer, house–sitting for my aunt. I leave when she comes back at the end of the summer.'

His handsome face showed his disappointment, but he didn't say anything.

She called after him. 'Did you notice something tonight?'

He paused and frowned.

'Despite all the silliness of this evening, including rolling around in my garden, you never once cracked a smile.'

He gave her a thoughtful look. Yes, she was probably right.

'See you in the morning, Cuan. Cake knives at dawn.'

She went inside and closed the door. He didn't hear her lock it.

Cuan headed back to his cottage. Before going inside he looked down the esplanade. He thought about Mhairi, the stubborn quilt saver, in that pretty dress of hers and wished he'd smiled more.

CHAPTER THREE

Seahorses and Sugarcraft

Mhairi tore the envelope open and read the letter from Cuan.

No wonder he didn't want her to read it. How arrogant and conceited he was. He'd offered her the chance to renege on the challenge, reminding her how stubborn she'd been accepting it. If she wanted to cancel, it was fine. How magnanimous he sounded.

Then she smiled to herself. He'd concluded with an invitation to have dinner with him. No details of where, when or why.

This was probably the main reason he didn't want her to read it.

She folded the letter, put it back in the envelope, and tucked it into her pattern folder. One to keep for the archives.

She went to sleep with thoughts of Cuan's taut physique pressed against her. It was unlikely she'd get involved with him. But she could dream, couldn't she?

Her second alarm went off in the morning. She'd slept through the first one. It didn't mean she was late, but breakfast wasn't an option. Getting herself showered, dressed and the cake presentable were the only priorities she had time for.

Hurrying out of the cottage carrying the cake in the largest box, she made her way to the post office. Another bright morning beckoned.

After the challenge, they'd all eat cake and exchange gossip. Surely someone had seen her and Cuan last night, if not rolling in the bushes, walking along the esplanade. Her actions would need to be explained over copious amounts of tea and chocolate cake.

She wore a blue calico dress and toning gingham pumps. She'd pinned her hair up to keep it from dangling in the ganache, and because it was easier than trying to tame it after her shower.

Ethel saw her and waved. They went into the post office together.

'I've set up a table for your cakes,' the postmaster said, sounding excited at the prospect of pandemonium in the post office. She really loved the people in this community. Where else could you buy a stamp, fresh baked treacle scones, a whipped ice cream cone and challenge a chocolatier? Nowhere she'd ever been. How she'd miss this place when she had to leave.

She pushed all unhappy thoughts aside and set up her cake, lifting it carefully from the box.

'Where did you get that lovely cake box?' Ethel asked her. 'It looks as though the cardboard is embossed.'

'It is. It's one of Cuan's boxes.'

'Did you steal that from him as well?' asked Ethel.

'No, he gave it to me last night. I met him while out strolling on the esplanade.'

The postmaster snorted. 'A little bird told me the two of you got up to a whole lot more than strolling by the sea.'

Mhairi blushed as bright as the pink sugarcraft roses on her cake.

Ethel waited for an explanation. Mhairi pretended to fuss with the cake, setting it on the silver foil cake board and adjusting the sugar paste flowers on top.

Ethel turned to the postmaster for the details.

'I heard that the grocer was leaving his shop very late last night, and saw Cuan canoodling with you on your front lawn,' said the postmaster 'You were both rolling about in the bushes. He could hear you giggling a mile off.'

Ethel adjusted her spectacles. 'Is this true, Mhairi?'

'No, yes, sort of, but it's slanted.'

'What angle is slanted?' the postmaster asked her. 'The angle Cuan had you pinned down while he lay on top of you?'

'The whole episode is taken out of context,' Mhairi insisted.

'That's why we need the details,' said Ethel. 'So. . . did you take a tumble with the chocolatier in your garden?'

Cuan spoke up. 'She made a grab for me, I fell backwards, and then she landed on top of me.' He'd entered again without them noticing.

Ethel continued her questioning. 'If Mhairi fell on top of you, why were you lying on top of her? Is her garden at an angle? Did you roll across the lawn?'

'We changed positions,' said Cuan. 'We started with Mhairi on top.'

The postmaster sniggered.

'The positions we'd landed in,' Cuan clarified. 'Not other types of. . . intimate positions.'

'I heard you were both pretty intimate,' said the postmaster. 'Playing kiss chase were you?'

Mhairi cast a curveball into the conversation. 'You'll know about that,' she said to the postmaster, 'because you're always chasing after Ethel's tail.'

Ethel tightened her lace weight knit shawl. 'He's the one who does all the chasing, not me.'

Mhairi gave Ethel a knowing smile. 'Sometimes he catches you, doesn't he?'

'I'm still fit, but not as brisk on my feet as I used to be,' said Ethel. 'My comfy brogues aren't made for running.'

'You said at the sewing bee you could outrun the postmaster if you wanted to,' Mhairi reminded her.

The postmaster grinned. 'Did she indeed? So you enjoy being caught by me, Ethel?'

'Right. . . let's get this challenge started,' said Ethel.

'My cake is outside in the car.' Cuan left to fetch it.

A handful of others arrived to witness the challenge, including Hilda, Judith and two ladies from the sewing bee.

Cuan carried in his cake. It was carefully wrapped in two large boxes. He set the two–tier, chocolate masterpiece up on the table.

He looked pleased with himself, Mhairi thought, looking at the elaborate chocolate twirls on his cake. It was impressive. She should never have accepted Cuan's challenge. She wished she hadn't. She also wished he wasn't so handsome and hard to resist. She intended to resist him. She really did.

Everyone involved was assembled in the post office. Paper plates were ready.

'Will I do the honours?' Ethel had a cake knife ready to slice into Mhairi's cake.

Mhairi's hands were shaking slightly from a horrible mix of nerves and excitement. 'Thanks, Ethel.'

On the whole, Cuan's cake looked the most impressive, but Mhairi's was so perfectly traditional, like a vintage chocolate cake, it was a matter of personal preference. When cut, the chocolatier's cake lost some of its impressive artistry, while Mhairi's chocolate cake sat firm, each layer holding its own against the master. The ganache glistened under the lights.

Cuan looked impressed with Mhairi's effort.

Everyone tasted the cakes. Some preferred Cuan's cake, others voted for Mhairi's old–fashioned chocolate cake.

Cuan had yet to sample it. He was the last to try it. Mhairi watched, wondering how he'd react.

'This tastes delicious.'

'I'm a quilter, not a baker, so I'll take that as an enormous compliment,' she said.

'Mhairi's cake gets my vote,' said the postmaster. 'My tastes are probably less sophisticated than some. I'm not partial to all the different bursts of flavour in the chocolatier's cake — cherry, vanilla, and quite a bitter chocolate. I enjoy a full–on chocolate experience and that old–fashioned cake is yummy.'

'Let's call it a draw,' said Cuan. He glanced at Mhairi. 'And never do anything like this again.'

Mhairi wondered if he'd held back on what he was truly capable of to give her a fair chance.

'I have a busy schedule today, so I'll leave you all to it,' said Cuan, heading for the door.

'Don't you want to take your cake with you?' said the postmaster.

'No, cut it up and give it out to your customers.'

Cuan left the shop, causing the coldest breeze they'd felt that day. The morning was a sizzler.

Mhairi worked with the cottage windows wide open. She fussy cut numerous pieces for a quilt that was ordered for framing.

She was thinking of stopping for lunch when she saw Cuan walk up and knock on the cottage door.

He wasn't smiling.

'I found another quilt. I've been clearing out a cupboard and this is the last quilt I assure you. I need the space for my work. I assumed the quilts belonged to the previous occupier, though they were on the top shelve of a cupboard, so perhaps they're from an older era, especially as they're vintage. I put them in the summerhouse, but then decided I had no need for them. Then I found this one. I thought you would want it.' He thrust it at her.

'Oh yes, this is lovely.' She ran her hands across the folded quilt. 'It's genuine vintage. Look at the stitching.' She hurried through to compare it to the other quilts he'd given her, leaving Cuan standing at the door.

He stepped inside.

Piles of carefully folded fabric pieces were on the table and shelves in the lounge, which was more like a sewing room. They'd been arranged by colour. Rolls of batting sat on the shelves alongside backing fabrics, mainly cottons.

'Is this what you do all day? Sew quilts?'

'Yes.'

'And you make a living from this?'

'I do. Not in your league, but it's a fair living for working at something I love. I'm building my business, and if my quilt designs become popular I could do quite well for myself. A home accessory company purchased two of my fabric designs last season. They'll be available in the shops throughout the country soon on bed linen and home decor items.'

This seemed to be of great interest to him. 'And you don't regret selling them your designs so they can use them for their own products?'

'Of course not. It's good business. It helps my income and gets my name out there as a designer.'

She stood on her tiptoes to reach the three quilts on the cupboard shelf.

Cuan stretched over her and lifted them down. She felt his body press against hers for the briefest moment, and her senses flared into overdrive.

He'd rolled up the sleeves of his cream linen shirt to reveal strong, leanly muscled forearms. His coffee–coloured trousers were belted and emphasised his taut torso. He looked so classy — and sexy. A lethal combination, especially when it was just the two of them alone in the cottage. Despite the windows being open and the sea breeze wafting in, Mhairi felt she needed more air to breathe.

'Are you okay?' he said.

'Yes, I just need a cold drink. I was about to have a glass of iced lemonade when you arrived. I've hardly stopped sewing all morning.'

Cuan put the quilts down, grasped her by the shoulders and sat her down on her chair by the window. Her work table was covered in fussy cut pieces for the quilt she'd been making.

He found his way through to the kitchen. She heard the fridge door open, the clink of glasses and the lemonade being poured. 'Do you want ice in yours?'

'Yes please. There's a stack of ice cubes in the freezer compartment.'

Cuan added the ice and brought two glasses through. 'Here, take a sip of this. Slowly, don't gulp it down. You're probably a bit dehydrated. You should make a point of having something to drink, even tea, in warm weather like this.'

He was fussing over her, something she wasn't used to. The previous men in her life were selfish prats and didn't know the meaning of being kind and caring. Perhaps Cuan wasn't such a grumpy pants after all?

'Feeling better? You don't look quite so flushed.'

He sat on the edge of her work table, displaying long, athletic thighs, unintentionally of course.

She drank down her lemonade in an effort to stay cool — and not from the hot weather.

He touched her hand and pulled the glass away from her lips. 'Easy there, tiger. Take a sip at a time.'

Phew! It was getting really hot in here.

Thankfully, the iced lemonade did its work and although Cuan remained close to her, her cheeks didn't feel quite so rosy.

'You're looking better already.'

She smiled tightly. Oh if only he knew.

He studied the quilt and pieces of fabric on the table. 'I like these seahorses. I love the sea. Are you going to sew them on to the quilt?'

'I am. I've fussy cut around them—'

'Fussy cut?'

'Cut around the edges of the seahorses that were printed on to fabric. The outlines are quite finicky and I use these fine scissors rather than my rotary cutter to snip around them carefully.'

She heard herself prattling on about quilting and stopped.

'What's wrong?'

'I don't want to bore you with the intricacies of quilt making.'

'No, please continue. I'm interested. I like the artistry in this. I can see the appeal even though I've never sewn anything, and don't have a yearning to either. But I can appreciate the work that goes into this and why you'd love doing it.' He glanced out at the sea. 'Especially with a view like this.'

She gazed out at the sun sparkling off the water and the bright cobalt sky. 'I've heard it's wonderful here in winter with storm grey skies sweeping across the shore and snow covering the fields, but I've always loved the summer, particularly June. It has always been a happy month.'

He gazed down at her. 'Are you happy, Mhairi? Happy here in the cottage, on your own?'

'Yes.' There was no hesitation, for this was true. 'I enjoy the freedom and I visit my aunt fairly often, especially in the summer months, and it's a welcome break from flat sharing with two other girls in the city. We all get on okay, but there's no real privacy.' She glanced up at him. 'Here, I can be myself, a manic quilter, making my own hours. If I want to get up at dawn and sew seahorses or work into the twilight hours, I can do it without disturbing anyone. I like the sense of freedom in that. And when I want company, there are the people who live around here. Ethel, Hilda, Judith and other ladies from the local sewing bee are like extended family.'

'But you'll be leaving at the end of the summer?'

'I will.' She shrugged. 'I couldn't stay even if I wanted to. There's only one bedroom and it's my aunt's room.' She explained about sleeping on the sofa. 'It's fine for a week's holiday but not as a permanent place to stay. So I'll have to go back to the city, but if my quilt business and fabric designs do well, I'll be able to visit more often.'

'Remember to visit me.'

'You're sort of unforgettable.'

'That's the nicest thing you've said to me.'

'Better than horrible insults.'

He suddenly seemed to realise how close they were sitting. He stood up and went over to admire rolls of fabric on a shelf. 'What type of fabric is this?'

'Voile. It's quite sheer. Ideal for creating a sea foam effect on the seascape quilts for framing.'

'And this?'

'Top quality cotton.'

He ran his fingers along the length of a role of white fabric printed with little red, white and blue sail boats. 'This feels lovely.'

'That's poplin. It's comparable to my quilting cottons.'

'What would you make with this, apart from quilts?'

'Various items. I made these quilted cushion covers from a similar poplin recently.' She got up and unfolded one of the cushion covers to show him. She quickly stuffed a cushion filler in it and sat it on the sofa.

'I like that. How many do you have?'

'They're a set of six, each one different but with a coastal theme.'

'Are they for sale?'

'Yes, but—'

'I want them. And six of the cushions. They'll be ideal for the summerhouse chairs.'

Cuan left with two bags full of cushions. He seemed delighted. She walked with him to the front door which was wide open.

'Your chocolate cake really was delicious,' he said in a hushed tone.

She smiled at him.

He almost smiled back.

'Careful,' she warned him. 'Don't spoil your track record for not smiling.'

He smirked.

'That's an improvement. Better than a sneer, but not quite a smile.'

He tried not to grin.

She laughed lightly. 'Thanks for. . . bringing me the lemonade.'

'It's no big deal.'

She shook her head. 'If you knew my past record with men, believe me, it's a big deal. Huge.'

He went to walk away and stopped. 'You read the letter, didn't you?'

'I did.'

His firm lips pressed together as if he was considering whether to say something or not and decided on the latter. He continued on.

'Are you a man who reneges on his offers?' she called to him.

He stopped and looked round at her. 'No, I'm not.'

She nodded firmly. 'Okay then.'

He almost smiled, knowing what she meant. 'Shall we say eight o'clock this evening?'

'Eight. I'll pop along.'

'Anything you'd like for dinner?'

'Surprise me.'

Cuan not only smiled, but laughed. 'You really shouldn't have said that.'

He walked away.

Never one to flinch from a challenge, as she'd already proved, Mhairi wondered what he had in mind — and if something more would be on the menu from him than just dinner.

CHAPTER FOUR

Mermaids and Meringues

Bunting fluttered along the length of the esplanade in the evening light. Soon it would be the summer fete. Mhairi was taking part with a quilting stall at the busy annual occasion. Many of the women from the sewing bee were participating. Hilda had spoken to Mhairi about coordinating their two stalls. Hilda's quilting products comprised of a wide variety of quilting items including bags, table runners, tea cosies and laptop bags as well as quilts for bedding. Mhairi's quilt stall would have a selection of her traditional quilts, art quilts and cushion covers. They really didn't clash, but the ladies tended to avoid competing and preferred to help each other in their crafting businesses.

It was almost eight at night. A sultry heat created a perfect June evening. Mhairi had thought about wearing the tea dress that the dressmaker had sewn, perhaps with magic in the stitches, but she didn't feel it was the right occasion. She hung it in the wardrobe and instead opted for a light and airy, little white broderie anglaise dress.

As she walked up to the chocolatier's cottage, she saw him outside the front door — and there was a woman with him, very attractive, early thirties, fashionably dressed more for the city than the seaside, and she was flirting with Cuan and flicking her silky auburn hair. Mhairi heard the woman's light laughter drift towards her and felt like retreating back home to the safety of her cottage where her heart would not be in jeopardy. But Cuan saw her and so she continued on, trying not to look dejected. After all, she wasn't actually dating Cuan. He'd invited her to have dinner. Nothing more, though she'd somehow let herself think that it could be the start of a relationship with him. That's when she realised she'd done it again — left herself vulnerable to disappointment. She didn't want Cuan to know this, and hoped her casual expression of acceptance of the situation shielded her true feelings.

'Mhairi, this is Vanessa.'

Vanessa glanced at her, clearly annoyed by the interruption.

'Vanessa is the marketing executive for the hotel group who are buying my new collection of luxury chocolates for their hotel restaurants.'

Mhairi smiled, fake as hell, but a smile nonetheless.

Cuan finished the introductions. 'Mhairi is a quilter.'

A carefully manicured hand reached out to Mhairi, and Vanessa gave her a condescending smile. 'A little quilter. How quaint.'

Mhairi shook hands with the hard–nosed marketing executive.

Cuan held an empty chocolate box, a prototype for the hotel's new product based on his recipes. He showed it to Mhairi. 'Vanessa brought a sample of the new packaging they've designed for the chocolates. You're a designer, what do you think?'

His voice was strained, but the look he gave her made her realise all the flirting was on Vanessa's part. She took the box and glanced at Cuan, searching his face for proof that he really did want her opinion on it. It was a classy chocolate box, and she liked the rich cream, gold and hazelnut brown colouring. His name was listed after the ingredients, like a cursory acknowledgment.

'It's very nice,' said Mhairi.

Cuan sensed there was something else. 'But?'

Mhairi shrugged. 'Your name is rather small, and being printed in gold–coloured lettering, I can hardly read it. If I didn't know your name, I probably wouldn't know what it said.'

Vanessa jumped in to defend the design. 'Cuan's name is perfectly clear. The lettering is subtle.'

Mhairi shook her head. 'The print looks less than a standard twelve–point. Probably a ten. Personally, I'd use a minimum of a sixteen–point print in gold. Certainly no less than a fourteen, and only then if the print was dark brown or black.' She handed the box to Cuan. His expression was a mix of admiration and delight that she'd stymied Vanessa.

Unwilling to back down, Vanessa grabbed the box from Cuan. She stabbed a finger at his name and glared at Mhairi. 'There's nothing wrong with the print size. What are you, some sort of print–size expert?' Vanessa's tone bore nothing but disdain.

'I worked in advertising years ago before becoming a quaint little quilter.'

She sensed those manicured hands wanted to throttle her. Mhairi continued. 'It seems silly to pay Cuan for his expertise, to use his

33

name as part of your new product, then diminish what you've paid for, rather than use it to full advantage to promote the fact that a master chocolatier created the chocolates.'

Cuan smiled. The best smile Mhairi had seen on his handsome face.

No smiles from Vanessa, just an uppity attitude and a snippy retort. 'I'll speak to management and product design and get back to you next week. Goodnight, Cuan.'

No goodnight for the little quilter.

Vanessa got into her car and drove off, gears crunching.

Mhairi wondered if she'd earned her dinner or had stepped way over the mark.

Cuan was still smiling at her. 'I hope you're hungry.'

'I am.'

He welcomed her in. 'It's such a warm night, I thought we could dine in the summerhouse.'

'Great.'

He led the way through the kitchen where the delicious aroma of dinner cooking in the kitchenette oven made her glad she'd resisted eating earlier so she'd be ready for whatever Cuan had made. She hadn't expected he'd have the oven on during a scorching night, but he didn't seem perturbed. A cooling system ensured there was a reasonable temperature, and so she thought she'd relax in the summerhouse while he served up dinner.

The doors to the summerhouse were open wide, allowing the evening air to waft in. He'd set a table, and arranged two chairs with the new cushions. Soft lighting gave a magical glow.

'This is lovely, Cuan,' she called to him. The kitchen door was open and she could see him moving around, efficiently serving up whatever he'd made.

'I'm glad you're pleased — and thanks for telling Vanessa what you thought of the design. I wouldn't have considered that, but I think you're right.'

'At least you're smiling.'

'She turned up uninvited,' he explained, carrying out a tray with two roast chicken dinners. A selection of fresh vegetables and chocolate sauce were expertly served on the plates. 'I made my favourite savoury chocolate sauce as an accompaniment.'

She tasted the sauce. 'Wow! This is delicious.'

'Red onions and a hint of chilli gives the chocolate a sweet and savoury flavour.'

'You've certainly surprised me.'

He looked pleased. 'If you enjoy it, I'll make us chocolate truffle pasta another night.'

She smiled at him. 'Another night?'

'Unless you insult me horribly by the end of this evening and we decide never to see each other again.'

'No insults. I'm on my best behaviour, especially if there's a future promise of chocolate truffle pasta.'

He gave her a wickedly sexy grin. 'Not too good behaviour?'

She blushed. 'Stop making me blush. I'm relishing dinner. This roast chicken is superb.'

'Scottish heather honey is part of the glaze,' he said proudly.

'I didn't expect to be eating a roast dinner on a hot night, but it's perfect.' She gazed around at the summerhouse — and at Cuan. 'Really perfect.'

An oven pinged.

'Excuse me. The meringues are ready. I'll take them out of the oven and let them cool.'

'Meringues?'

'Chocolate of course,' he called from the kitchen. 'With whipped cream and strawberries, served with cinder toffee. My own recipe. It's tipsy with Scottish whisky.'

'You're spoiling me.'

'And rightly so.'

With the meringues cooling in the kitchen, Cuan came back and they ate the remainder of their dinner together, chatting about cake boxes, chocolate recipes, mermaid quilt motifs and meringues.

'I can't remember the last time I've enjoyed myself so much,' said Mhairi.

'Me too. We should do this often, before you have to leave.'

She smiled warmly. 'I'd like that, Cuan.'

He took a deep breath. 'The whole business deal with the hotel group is the reason for my lack of smiles. Not making excuses, but after I signed the deal, which was right in the midst of buying this cottage, I had my doubts — had I sold out?'

Mhairi shook her head. 'You haven't sold out at all. You've extended your own brand, linking it with another certainly, but that's how to expand.'

'You've got quite a good head for business.'

'So I've been told. I think I'm just practical. I don't hold on to my designs with hoops of steel. I want my designs, my quilts, my crafts out there so that people can buy them and hopefully enjoy them. I don't see the point in making something and then hiding it away, being precious about it.' She shrugged. 'I've always felt that way.'

'I've felt the opposite, so I'm glad of your influence. I like to keep control of my recipes, my work, but if I want to expand I'll have to let go a little.'

'If you don't, you won't have time for anything.'

'Such as dinner on a beautiful night like this with a beautiful woman.'

Mhairi blushed.

'You blush a lot.'

'It's mainly your fault, but ask me that tomorrow and I'll probably deny it.'

He smiled at her, and in the glow of the summerhouse, she noticed what a great smile Cuan had.

He cleared away the plates and brought the meringues out to the summerhouse.

Mhairi tasted a piece of chocolate meringue. It melted in her mouth.

'Thumbs up?' Cuan asked her.

'Definitely. You're certainly in the right business.'

'As are you. These cushions are ideal.'

'Tell me more about your work,' she said. 'I noticed you have books on all sorts of flavours you add to your chocolate cakes and sweets. Do you ever make your own chocolate?'

'No. I don't actually make chocolate. I use chocolate to make things.'

'It must be interesting experimenting with different flavours.'

'Yes, it is. I suppose it's like your quilting. There's always another new taste combination to use in the recipes. I've been working a lot recently with salt caramel chocolate. It's very versatile and delicious with both milk chocolate and dark chocolate cake toppings.'

'Do you think you'll settle here at the cottage?'

'That's my plan. During the past, I travelled extensively, learning new techniques, discovering different flavours, but I always come back to Scotland. This feels like home. I considered living in one of the cities like Edinburgh or Glasgow, but then I thought — where would I really like to live? And it was in a cottage by the sea. So when this became available, I snapped it up.' He looked out at the garden. 'I'm adding an extension though to give me an extra room. I noticed Ethel's cottage had one and the cottages are alike.'

'Ethel's extension is ideal. We have our sewing bee in her cottage. The ladies used to meet once or twice a week in one of the other cottages. That was before I arrived. Ethel said she's happy to hold it at her cottage now.'

'I overheard ladies at the post office saying there had been two marriages and engagements locally in the past year.'

'Yes, romance is definitely in the sea air.'

He looked at her with such affection she felt inclined to get up and wander out into the garden.

She gazed up at the stars in the clear night sky. 'It really is a lovely evening. Quite magical.'

'What's this I hear about the dressmaker sewing spells into the clothes she makes?'

'It's not spells. Not that I've ever heard. It's just a sort of local knowing that the dressmaker sews magic into her dresses. True or not, it's a nice idea. She sent a dress to me recently. A lovely vintage dress with a rose print. Her assistant, Judith, gave it to me. You met Judith at the post office.'

He nodded.

'Apparently I'll know when the time is right to wear the dress. I considered putting it on this evening, then changed my mind and wore this broderie anglaise.'

He smiled broadly. 'I'll have to learn all these fancy fabric names.'

'Why? You don't need to.'

'I do if we're to be. . . friends. I'd like to understand what you do so we can talk about things.'

A shiver of excitement shot through her. He was making an effort to understand her work. Did men like him exist? She'd never met them. Not in her world.

'You've got that wistful look again.'

She breathed in the warm, fragrant air. 'I was just thinking. . . '

'Thinking what?' he prompted her.

Thinking of how gorgeous and perfect you are. She smiled to herself, and a pale blush started to form on her cheeks.

'Wicked thoughts, Mhairi?'

She smiled and walked over to the roses. 'I'm on my best behaviour, remember?'

He nodded. 'More tea? We can drink it inside, and I'll show you how to fill a chocolate truffle shell.'

They headed inside. 'I think you're luring me in for other reasons.'

'Dubious reasons?'

She nodded. 'Dark and devious.'

'Whatever could those be?'

'You want to teach me your tricks of the trade so I can become your chocolatier apprentice. Then you'll be able to leave me working over a hot stove of melted chocolate while you go swimming in the sea.'

He sighed heavily. 'Scuppered again.'

They fooled around in the kitchen until almost midnight. Mhairi did learn some tricks from Cuan, including how to sculpt chocolate leaves and dip fresh cherries into melted chocolate. He showed her a tray of milk chocolate truffle shells waiting to be filled with his special mix. Filling them wasn't easy, but she gave it her best shot.

She also learned what a milk chocolate kiss tasted like when he kissed her gently after she'd sampled a spoonful of truffle mix.

He held her close, and she felt his lean muscled body press against her. 'What do you think?'

'Totally delicious, but perhaps I should try again with the white chocolate truffle mix?'

He nodded firmly. 'You're right. You should.' He reached over, picked a white truffle from a tray and gave it to her.

'Mmm, this tastes perfect.'

He smiled down at her, and then kissed her.

He nodded. 'I agree. Perfect.'

Then he kissed her again, and for several moments, she was lost to the longing caresses of Cuan.

He didn't take things further, and she was glad. He seemed to understand that if they were to have any sort of future together, he needed to take things slowly with her.

The kitchen clock chimed softly.

'It's midnight, Cuan. I'd better go. Thanks for dinner. This evening was. . . unforgettable.'

And so was Mhairi. Since the first time he'd seen her, confronted in the post office with his ridiculous wanted poster, he couldn't get her out of his thoughts. No woman had affected him like this before. Had he finally found the woman who was right for him? He hoped so.

CHAPTER FIVE

Crochet Kisses

Cuan walked Mhairi home.

They passed by Ethel's cottage and Cuan wanted to know how the extension looked from inside.

'You should drop by sometime,' said Mhairi. 'I'm sure Ethel would be delighted to see you. She's very happy with her extension. It has allowed her to dedicate a whole area to the spinning while keeping her knitting workspace and selection of yarns separate. She knits amazing shawls and scarves. Some are traditional patterns, and others are the latest fashions. Both ranges sell well.'

'Are you sure she wouldn't mind if I just dropped by?'

'You'll be treated to tea and pieces of Ethel's special shortbread.'

'I'll pop round tomorrow. The sooner I make a firm decision on the extension and get it started the better. The cottage came with planning permission to build a back garden extension. I don't want the builders working on it in the winter. Autumn and winter are my busiest times and especially Christmas.'

'Ethel will give you all the details you need, and probably recommend the local lads who built it. They work quick and she said there was very little fuss to the community.'

'Excellent.'

They arrived outside Mhairi's cottage.

Was he going to give her a goodnight kiss?

She was still wondering when he pulled her into his arms and kissed her with enough passion to make her swoon.

'Are you okay, Mhairi?' he said.

'It's just the hot night.' It wasn't quite a lie, only a slant on the truth. The evening was a scorcher, but the effect Cuan had on her burned just as hot.

He grinned, and she sensed he knew.

'Have a glass of that cold lemonade,' he said. 'That worked earlier.'

She smiled at him. Oh, yes, he definitely knew she'd swooned.

'Goodnight, Mhairi.' There was a hint of laughter in his voice.

Quilting kept Mhairi busy all morning. Summer sea fog billowed past the window. As usual, it was open wide and the warmth wafted in. It was the first morning in ages she hadn't been treated to a view of Cuan's daily dip. Everything was misted over, but she assumed being a creature of aquatic habit, he'd been for a swim.

Of course, she now had something more to think about than Cuan's hot bod while she was working. She'd replayed the events from the previous night, especially the parts where he'd kissed her — and sewn an applique rose on to a quilt without hardly realising.

Her phone rang. It was Ethel.

'I'm boiling the kettle in the kitchen, so I don't think he can hear me,' she said in a hushed tone.

Mhairi had been so deep in her own thoughts she didn't quite grasp what Ethel was talking about.

'The chocolatier's here,' Ethel whispered anxiously. 'I've got him in my extension looking at my yarn.'

She made it sound as if she had him trapped like a butterfly in a net. A local species meriting scrutiny.

'He's brought a tape measure. I don't mind him standing on my work table to measure how high the extension is, but he's wearing a pair of shorts, and I'm telling you, that man's got a great pair of pins on him. I didn't know where to look. And he keeps talking about *you*.'

There was a rustling noise in the background, then Ethel said into the phone, 'Yes, your yarn order will be posted out this afternoon. Bye.' And she hung up.

Mhairi wondered whether to pop along to Ethel's cottage or hide under the quilt she was sewing until Cuan had left. She hadn't built a quilt fort in a long time.

The phone rang again.

'Get your tail over here, Mhairi.'

Click, and Ethel had gone.

Mhairi tidied her hair and added a touch of lipstick in a soft pink that matched the cotton dress she was wearing. In winter, she lived in trousers and leggings, but in the summer, she had a selection of dresses that were easy to wash, comfy to wear and made her feel like she was on holiday. She'd sewn them herself from three trusty

41

patterns. With so many beautiful fabrics around, it was great to use the lovely cotton prints to run up these little dresses in her sewing machine.

She looked around for a suitable excuse.

She'd been crocheting a fashionable shawl, so she picked up the crochet hook and yarn and hurried along to pretend to ask Ethel's expert advice on how to create a lovely edging.

Armed with crochet, Mhairi ventured into Ethel's cottage. The front door was open and she heard Cuan talking about delicious shortbread.

'Oh, sorry to interrupt, Ethel. I was working on this new shawl and wondered if you had any tips for the edging stitches, but I can come back later.' She nodded and smiled acknowledgement to Cuan who was indeed standing on Ethel's work table measuring the extension from every angle.

Ethel handed Cuan up another piece of shortbread.

When he saw Mhairi he jumped down, tapped the last measurement into his phone and emailed the statistics to himself.

'I want to make sure the roof will be suitable for air vents. An ambient room temperature is vital for my cakes and confectionary.'

Ethel gave Mhairi a glazed look and then went through to the kitchen. 'Come away in, Mhairi. We're just having another wee cup of tea.'

'Seeing Ethel's work room has given me lots of ideas,' he enthused to Mhairi.

Seeing Cuan in those shorts and snug T–shirt gave Mhairi lots of ideas too. None of which she would ever reveal.

Cuan ran over to the far corner of the extension. 'This is bigger than I thought. Size really matters.'

Mhairi heard Ethel quip from the kitchen. 'That's what most men say, but it's what you do with it that matters.'

Cuan agreed, hearing her too, but not quite getting her meaning. He continued to enthuse. 'The proportions are ideal. I could fit a cooker, fridge and chiller in here and still have tons of space available for my tables and work surfaces. I could even squeeze in a display cabinet for my truffles.'

Mhairi nodded, trying not to laugh. 'Great,' she said. 'I'll just help Ethel bring the tea through.'

Cuan whipped out his measuring tape and starting sizing up the width of the windows.

Excessive giggling erupted from the kitchen.

'Is everything okay?' Cuan called to them.

Mhairi helped Ethel carry through the tea and shortbread.

'Yes,' said Mhairi. 'Ethel was showing me where I went wrong with crocheting my chain stitches.'

Ethel went along with the ruse, rather than let Cuan know they'd been giggling about him. 'When you do your yarn over, make sure you have three stitches on your hook. It'll make all the difference to the finished pattern.'

Cuan accepted another cup of tea to wash down his shortbread. 'I'm all fired up now. This is going to work so well. I'll give those builders a call and get the ball rolling.'

'They're clean, tidy and fast workers,' Ethel told him.

'I'll tell them you recommended them,' he said.

They all sat down and drank their tea.

Mhairi tried not to look at Cuan's athletic thighs. The fabric of his shorts was pulled taut across them as he sat on the edge of an armchair within touching distance of her. She was sure he hadn't intended causing her heart rate to double.

Ethel looked at Mhairi over the rim of her cup. 'Cuan was telling me you loved his meringues last night.'

Mhairi cleared her throat, almost choking on her tea. 'Yes, they were outstanding. We had dinner in the summerhouse.'

'I bought quilted cushions from Mhairi. They're great for the chairs in the summerhouse.'

'It sounds as if you're planning to settle here permanently,' Ethel said to him.

He glanced at Mhairi. 'I am. I've been a bit standoffish since I arrived. Apologies for that. I've had work matters on my mind, but Mhairi has helped settle those in all sorts of ways.'

Ethel grinned. 'Has she now?'

'Yes. A chocolate box for a new product is being redesigned as we speak because of Mhairi's designer know–how and input.'

Ethel looked right at him. 'Be careful not to let her slip through your fingers. Young women like Mhairi don't come along very often. We'll certainly all miss her when she goes back to the city.'

Cuan frowned. 'We should find a way to encourage her to stay. What do you say, Ethel?'

Ethel nodded.

Mhairi blushed, gulped down her tea and got up to leave. 'Thanks for the crochet advice, Ethel.'

'Are you busy this evening?' Cuan asked Mhairi.

'I am. It's the sewing bee tonight.'

He smiled, nodded and accepted this. 'Probably just as well. I've a tricky chocolate croquembouche to tackle.'

'Good luck with that,' said Mhairi, heading out.

The sewing bee was buzzing with gossip about Mhairi's dinner date with Cuan and his antics in Ethel's extension.

One of the ladies sat sewing a wrap over skirt. 'Did he really wear shorts and stand on your table, Ethel?'

Ethel's arms were folded across her chest and she relaxed in her armchair in the hub of the bee. She nodded and gave a cheeky smile. 'I know he's sweet on Mhairi, but he certainly perked up my day.'

'No offence,' said Hilda, 'but what's made him become so. . . friendly all of a sudden?'

'He had a lot of business worries on his mind,' Ethel explained. 'But Mhairi's set him right about a few things, haven't you?'

Mhairi was now in the hot seat. Several sets of eager eyes waited on her revealing more gossip. She told them about Vanessa.

'The cheek of her!' said Judith. 'Sounds like a right madam.'

'She's probably after Cuan,' Ethel concluded. 'She'd turned up at his house uninvited.'

'It's okay for us to drop by each other,' said Hilda, 'but not an outsider like her.'

They all agreed.

'Cuan's up to his elbows in chocolate tonight,' said Ethel, 'or he'd be canoodling with Mhairi again.'

Mhairi stitched the edges of her seahorse motif on to a quilt. 'I've no plans for further canoodling as you put it.' She concentrated on her stitches.

'Don't tell lies,' Ethel scolded her nicely.

'All right, so I'm probably going to have dinner with him again soon,' Mhairi admitted.

'I wonder what he'll rustle up for you this time?' said Judith. 'I like the sound of his sweet and savoury chocolate sauce.'

'He mentioned he'd cook chocolate truffle pasta.'

'It has put me in the notion of cooking with chocolate,' said Hilda. 'Anyone got a recipe book?'

Several of the ladies said they had, and they agreed to collaborate and share their favourite chocolate–based recipes.

'I'd like the recipe for the chocolate cake you made,' Hilda said to Mhairi.

'I'll give you a copy,' said Mhairi.

Ethel pointed to the table where cakes, sandwiches and tea were set up. 'I forgot to mention. . . Cuan dropped off a big box of chocolates for our sewing bee evening. Help yourselves.'

Ethel didn't need to offer twice. The chocolates were passed around and shared.

Hilda savoured a champagne truffle. 'You'll have to keep dating the chocolatier, Mhairi, if he's going to lavish the sewing bee with treats like these.'

The women laughed, and continued their evening of sewing and other crafts — combined with gossip and delicious chocolates.

'Maybe we'll have another wedding here,' one of the ladies said, glancing at Mhairi.

Mhairi smiled and concentrated on her sewing.

The ladies spoke about the various couples who had met and fallen in love in the local area. Some had married, others were engaged.

'I think there's a sense of romance about living here,' said Ethel.

'It has become a hive of little cottage businesses,' Hilda remarked.

Mhairi agreed. 'I'm looking forward to the summer fete.'

'Our stalls are side by side,' said Hilda. 'We're hoping to offer a great selection of quilting items.'

'I'm having an extra stall this year to display my new yarns,' said Ethel. She pointed to a shelf stacked with knitted shawls, wraps and blankets. 'The other stall will display finished goods. They usually sell well.'

'I wonder if Cuan is taking part in the fete. Has anyone told him about it?' asked Mhairi.

No one had.

'It's advertised on the notice board in the post office,' said Ethel, 'but he may not have seen it. You should tell him, Mhairi.'

'I will. I'll tell him tomorrow.'

Mhairi was busy the next day. She carried several parcels of quilts to the post office ready for one of the main pick–ups by the courier service.

After dropping them off, she decided to walk along the esplanade towards Cuan's cottage. She didn't plan on dropping in, but if he saw her and waved her over she would be happy to go in. She'd tell him about the fete.

With thoughts of how much she liked him, she walked along the esplanade, admiring the sea and the bunting blowing in the warm breeze. Big Sam the silversmith went by on the far side of the road, and they gave each other an acknowledging wave.

She blinked against the sunlight shining off the water, and then glanced over at Cuan's cottage.

Her heart tightened when she saw Vanessa coming out of the cottage and standing at the front door with Cuan. Vanessa saw Mhairi and gave him a kiss on the cheek to ignite her jealousy.

Feeling hurt and upset, Mhairi hurried back to her cottage.

Vanessa smiled to herself, seeing Mhairi's reaction.

Cuan didn't see Mhairi at all, and she didn't see him wipe the kiss from his face as Vanessa drove off.

Cuan packed an overnight bag and tried a few times to phone Mhairi. He got no reply. He locked his cottage, put the bag in his car and drove down to her cottage. He knocked on the door.

Mhairi, her face still wet with tears, pretended she wasn't in.

Cuan drove off to the city, thinking he'd call her later. Perhaps she'd switched her phone off and was busy working on her quilts with the ladies from the sewing bee.

Ethel went to visit Mhairi the next morning.

'I can see you're upset, Mhairi. I came to tell you the gossip, but I suppose you've heard.'

They sat down in the lounge and Ethel told her what she'd heard.

'It's just gossip, but apparently Cuan has signed some sort of deal where he's agreed to work more closely with the marketing lady in the city.'

Mhairi was distraught. 'With Vanessa?'

Ethel nodded, and added fuel to the gossip. 'It sounds like an excuse to be mixing his chocolates in another bowl.' She pursed her lips in disapproval.

'Thanks for telling me, Ethel. I was a fool to think he was different from the men I've known in the past.'

'There are nice men out there. Give it time, you'll find the man for you one day.'

Ethel gave her a comforting hug. 'Come on, I'll make us a cuppa, and I'll help you with your quilting.'

During the day, Mhairi threw herself into her work and ignored a call and a text message from Cuan. She didn't want to talk to him or listen to his excuses. She'd been down that road too many times.

CHAPTER SIX

Cottage by the Sea

Aurora turned up at the cottage to visit Mhairi, and to pick up the quilt block design she was contributing to the latest issue of Aurora's online sewing, knitting and craft magazine.

Aurora, an attractive young woman with shiny chestnut hair and blue eyes, had moved from the city to live locally, and had married one of the men who owned a cottage within the community. She'd previously worked for a glossy magazine in London and had a classy appearance.

'I've got the quilt block design here.' Mhairi handed it to her.

'This is lovely. Flowers are always popular with our readers. I'm editing the features for the next issue which will highlight those taking part in the fete. Then in the following issue, I'll have lots of pics of the fete itself.'

'What are the top features this time in the magazine?'

Aurora sat down in the lounge. 'We're featuring a beautiful tea dress pattern by the dressmaker. Tea dress patterns are extremely popular, especially if they're easy to sew and wearable. One of the sewing bee ladies ran a sample up in a ditsy floral print and we're including pictures of her making it. This new pattern is one of the dressmaker's top designs, so the magazine will get quite a bit of coverage when people know it's available. She's given us dress patterns before. This is another classic wrap over so it fits various sizes. It's a flattering design with a pretty V–neckline.'

'The dressmaker is very generous.'

'She is,' Aurora agreed. 'There was a time when she thought I was nothing but a troublemaker, as trouble tends to follow me around, but we soon sorted out our differences, and now she's a regular part of the magazine.'

They went on to discuss other patterns being featured in the next issue.

'Hilda says her quilted beach bag is going to be featured.'

'It is. Lovely design. Hilda's contributing the pattern. I'd like to make one, but I've very little time at the moment with working on the magazine and settling in.'

'How is married life suiting you?'

Aurora's pretty face lit–up with happiness. 'It's great, but I married a wonderful man. I can't imagine going back to my old life in the city. I feel like I've been part of a couple for a long, long time, which isn't true, but that's how it feels. It's as if I've slotted into being a couple with him so easily.'

'Do you miss the city at all?'

'Not a bit of it. I have a bigger life here in this seaside community than I ever had in the city. And I lived in London. Of course, I'm originally from here, but that was years ago, and now I feel like I've come home.' Aurora smiled. 'Are you thinking of doing what I did — moving away from the city to live in a cottage by the sea?'

'I'm not sure. Things have unsettled me recently.'

Aurora had heard the gossip. 'The chocolatier heartbreaker?'

Mhairi sighed. 'It's my own fault for getting my hopes up with him. I never learn.'

'Don't. Never learn to close your heart. There's no happiness in that.'

Mhairi nodded. 'I downloaded and printed out a couple of the colouring pages from the last issue of your magazine. My aunt loves colouring books and she's got a nice set of pencils. I'm thinking of trying some colouring in to help me relax.'

'Do that, and I'll drop off some more pages for you to colour.'

Mhairi waved Aurora off, poured herself a glass of lemonade, and sat by the window, having a go at colouring in a seahorse in various shades of blues — and tried not to dwell on thoughts of Cuan.

Before making dinner, Mhairi decided to get some fresh air, but instead of walking along the esplanade, she went into the garden shed and used her aunt's vintage bicycle for a bit of exercise. The bike was painted eggshell blue and there was a basket on the front that was made for being filled with flowers or fresh bread and bakery goods.

49

Mhairi jumped on and cycled along the coastline, enjoying the sea breeze blowing through her hair and summery dress. She rode all the way along to the far point of the bay before turning around and heading back. She'd passed Cuan's cottage on the way by and saw a builders van parked outside. No sign of Cuan. She surmised he'd given the go ahead to start work on the extension. By the time she was heading back, the van had gone.

A mellow, early evening sun turned the sea to molten gold and gave every white and cream painted cottage a gilded appearance.

She parked the bike against the wall of her cottage and went in to make dinner.

The kitchen at the back was shaded and felt quite cool, so she threw some oven chips on to a baking tray and put them on to cook while she prepared a large mixed salad with a delicious dressing. She cut a slice of crusty bread, made a pot of tea and ate dinner in the lounge, watching the sun–burnished sea.

Cuan had hurt her, but she'd been hurt before. She'd get over him, and her time here at the cottage would become just another memory. And yet. . . she didn't want her time at the cottage to be tainted. She wanted the summer to stretch long, warm and last forever.

In the past when her relationships had soured, she'd phone her aunt for a chat. She remembered her aunt's advice. 'Indulge in whatever whimsy takes your fancy, Mhairi.'

She wasn't sure what whimsy she had a notion of. Maybe she'd think of one later.

Sometimes, her aunt would also say, 'Pack a bag for the weekend and get yourself over here. We'll quilt, knit and crochet ourselves into corkscrews, and watch films on the telly until we're square–eyed.'

She smiled at the memories, for they had done all these things.

The sea looked tempting for an evening swim, but not when she'd just had dinner. A dip in the water at night would have to wait.

Cuan checked the messages on his phone. Nothing from Mhairi. Should he be worried? If something had happened, Ethel would've contacted him. He put his phone in the pocket of his expensive dark suit and walked into the upmarket hotel restaurant where he had a meeting, a business dinner with Vanessa and some of the managers involved in the deal.

He was tempted to call Mhairi again, but didn't want to look desperate. Some women didn't like possessive men. He'd have to tough it out, and hope he could talk to her face to face when he got home.

Mhairi fell asleep on the sofa. It was almost dawn when she woke up. She showered and considered going to bed, but instead got dressed, had a cup of tea, an early breakfast of fresh fruit and cereal, and set about quilting.

At around nine in the morning, Ethel phoned Mhairi.

'The sewing bee ladies are having a get together at my house to organise things for the fete. Would you like to join us, or have you quilt orders to complete?'

'I'm well ahead with my work,' Mhairi said, but didn't mention she'd been up since dawn. 'I'll pop over in a few minutes.'

'I'll put the kettle on.'

Ethel's cottage was abuzz with activity.

Several sewing bee ladies were organising items for their various stalls. A sense of excitement filled the air. Ethel had a list of the stalls involved and the number was up again from the previous year. The postmaster was one of the main organisers of the annual event, and Ethel was helping ensure everyone pulled together to make it a success.

Ethel checked the list. 'Sewing and knitting are the dominant goods, as usual, but there's certainly a lot more variety in those. Vintage continues to have a strong influence on these, and I think the sales of vintage–style fabrics, fashions and knitting are going to be huge. Crochet is popular too.'

Ethel looked at Mhairi and Hilda, and others who intended selling quilted items. 'The stalls are going to be set up right along the main part of the esplanade, starting near the shops. The quilt stalls will be in the centre of the line–up with knitting and sewing stalls on either side. Last year we grouped similar stalls together and everyone reported an increase in sales, so we're doing the same again this year.'

'Mhairi and I are coordinating our stalls so that our quilting goods compliment each other,' said Hilda. 'But any other quilters are welcome to set up near us.'

A couple of quilters put their hands up, indicating they wanted to do this.

Ethel took a note of their names, and stall numbers were allocated.

Ione, spoke up. 'I've been quilting my new fairy doll items. Do you think I should have my stall next to the soft toys, sewing or quilting?'

'I'd put them next to Mhairi's quilting stall,' Ethel advised her. 'Those fairy dolls are adorable, and the quilted fairy cushions are so cute.'

Ione nodded, delighted, and was given a slip of paper with her stall number. She leaned over and studied the list. 'Where is Big Sam's silversmith stall?' Ione was engaged to Sam.

'Big Sam is just along from the jewellery stalls,' Ethel told her.

'That's great,' said Ione.

Ethel continued. 'Mairead is a botanical artist and quilter, but she's only selling her floral art this year. She's beside Tavion's flower stall. Tiree, the dressmaker's apprentice, is selling her beautiful new dress designs. The dressmaker, as usual, isn't having a stall, but she's made a financial contribution to the fete fund which will help pay for the marquees. During the day the marquees will supply visitors with snacks and refreshments, and in the evening will hold the fete party and dance. Two live bands have been hired.'

'Where are the baking stalls?' one of the women asked.

'Near the sewing stalls. Bredon the beemaster is selling his honey with the baking, and as far as we know the chocolatier isn't taking part in the fete.' Ethel put the list aside. 'So I think that's everyone in our wee circle sorted. Anyone else should contact the grocer or the postmaster for stall hire information.'

Hilda gave Ethel a cup of tea. She took a sip. 'The weather is set to be a scorcher for the fete, so keep that in mind. Oh and, Aurora will be filming the event and featuring the sewing, knitting, crochet, papercraft, colouring in and other crafts from those who participate in her magazine. The video will go up on her website, so if you want featured, speak to Aurora.'

Mhairi poured a cup of tea and sat down to talk to Ethel.

Ethel updated Mhairi on the building work being done on Cuan's cottage. 'I was chatting to one of the builders. He told me they're being paid to do the job quick. They moved the summerhouse in the back garden to make room for the extension.'

Mhairi was disappointed. 'The summerhouse was lovely.' She thought they were doing away with it.

'No, they're moving it to the opposite side of the garden to make more room for the extension which is similar in design to mine.'

'What about his rose garden?'

'The flower grower who tends to it says he'll replant a few rose bushes alongside the summerhouse,' Ethel explained. 'The garden will still be lovely, just shifted around a bit.'

'Cuan has tried to phone and text me,' Mhairi told her. 'But I haven't replied. I don't know what to say to him. I don't feel like talking.'

'Don't talk to him if you don't want to,' said Ethel.

'What would you do?'

Ethel sighed heavily. 'I'm not one for keeping my lips buttoned. I'd tell him exactly what I thought of him and his behaviour, but that's just me. I'm confrontational.'

After she left Ethel's cottage, Mhairi walked back along the esplanade. Stalls were being set up along with extra bunting. The sea looked so tempting. . .

Wearing a light blue swimsuit, Mhairi swam in the sea and enjoyed a day on the beach. The sunshine and fresh sea air made her feel better, and she planned to do this more often.

With her hair dripping wet, she wrapped a silky sarong around her waist, picked up her towel, stepped into her sandals and headed up from the shore to her cottage. And that's when she saw Cuan. He'd been watching her.

She kept walking to the cottage but he hurried after her.

'Mhairi, wait. What's wrong?'

She stopped and faced him. Her heart ached seeing him, looking so handsome.

She took a deep breath and let her feelings pour out. Armed with the knowledge he'd been in the city with Vanessa, she told him she didn't want to see him again.

He tried to defend himself but she was having none of it.

53

'I saw the two of you outside the cottage. I saw Vanessa kiss you.'

'You were watching?'

'I was walking nearby.'

He held up his hands. 'Vanessa kissed me, I didn't respond.'

'The two of you are obviously close.'

'We're not. It's just business.'

'It didn't look like business to me. She glanced over at me, delighted to let me see her kiss you. Do you normally let your business associates kiss you?'

'No, of course not, but. . .Vanessa can be manipulative. However, she's the one I have to deal with for this business contract.'

'It seems she likes to seal her deals with a kiss rather than a signed contract.'

'I signed the ruddy contract last night.'

Mhairi raised her eyebrows.

'I signed a new deal at a business dinner with Vanessa and other managers at the hotel restaurant. I told them I'd be working a lot more from the city.'

'I thought you were happy here, at the cottage. The builders have even started work on it.'

'I did it because of you. You wanted me to be more open to collaborations. It was because of your advice, and I thought it would be great as I'd be nearer you after the summer, and expanding my business.'

'You're blaming me?'

'No, but if you hadn't suggested a change in attitude, I wouldn't have fought for a new deal or looked for somewhere to live in the city.'

She shook her head. 'I don't feel comfortable with any of this.'

'I'm was planning to work there in the hope of being closer to you, keeping the cottage, but living between the city and the sea. I thought I could visit you in the city while working with the hotel people on the new range of chocolates. You're going to leave here at the end of the summer. I wanted to ask you to move in with me, but then I thought. . . I can't ask you to do that so quickly. You've been hurt in the past and I didn't want to pressurise you.'

54

Mhairi felt her world tilt. Was he telling the truth, or lying? She couldn't be sure. Her trust had been broken too many times in the past to take a chance on trusting Cuan so easily.

'I kept thinking this is going to come to an end when your aunt comes home. Even if you stayed with her, you can't sleep on the sofa forever.' He ran a frustrated hand through dark, silky hair. 'Things were going so well between us.'

'Yes, and then I hear you're going to go back to the city to work closer with Vanessa. I've only got the summer here.'

'I wasn't going to do it until the end of the summer.' He sounded exasperated.

His phone rang. He checked the caller. It was Vanessa. 'I've got to get this, it's the hotel.'

'No problem, we're done anyway.' She walked off.

Inside the cottage, she closed the door against the world, away from Cuan. She planned to go into work mode, get ready for the fete — and have nothing more to do with him.

Gossip soon circulated about her confrontation with Cuan.

Ethel phoned Mhairi.

'I heard you had an argument with him.'

'I did.'

'Did he deny her kissing him?'

'No, he didn't deny it. He blamed her for being manipulative, and me for encouraging him to change his attitude and expand his business.'

'Blaming everyone except himself.'

'I blame myself for thinking I could trust him.'

'What are you going to do?'

'Get my quilts ready for the fete. Focus on my work. Swim in the sea — and to blazes with romance.'

'Is he really going to live between here and the city?'

'So he says.'

'Midwinter the chocolatier tried that and failed.'

'I'm going to get on with what I want to do,' Mhairi said firmly. 'It's the fete this weekend, and with friends like you and the ladies from the sewing bee, I don't need the hassle of the chocolatier.'

Mhairi showered and settled down to sew her quilts. She could lose herself for hours, stitching, piecing together a beautiful design, working with scraps of fabric, creating something that could last a lifetime. She'd always loved her sewing. It cheered her up and never let her down.

She stopped to make a tasty dinner — cheese and tomato pizza and a crisp green salad. Plain by Cuan's standards, but far less complicated.

After dinner she continued to sew, working on a lovely seascape quilt, one for framing. She hand–stitched a starfish applique on to the quilt using aquamarine and sapphire blue thread.

The warm sea air poured into the lounge. With every stitch she forced herself to concentrate on her quilt and not think about Cuan.

Cuan's sleep was disturbed with difficult dreams. He couldn't get thoughts of Mhairi out of his mind.

He pictured her wearing the blue swimsuit that flattered her lovely figure and made him want to pull her close and kiss her. He wanted to reassure her of his loyalty. She could trust him. He knew that, but she didn't, and he wasn't sure how to convince her.

Then he thought about Vanessa. He had no romantic interest in her. She was a game player. He'd met people like her before. She was part of the business deal, but he didn't want her to ever kiss him again.

Unsettled, he got out of bed and went through to the kitchen for a cool drink of water. As he sipped it, he looked out the window at the back garden, and felt a pang of sadness when he saw the empty space where the summerhouse had been. Now it lay dismantled in a corner of the garden.

He thought of the happy evening he'd spent having dinner in the summerhouse with Mhairi. He could still hear her laughter and pictured her smiling at him. If he could rewind, he'd never have let her go.

He finished the water and glanced one more time at the summerhouse lying in pieces. It would be rebuilt soon. Could he do the same with his broken relationship with Mhairi? Building bridges when trust had been shattered was never easy, but perhaps there was another way to win her heart. He had to try.

CHAPTER SEVEN

Truffles and Trouble

The day of the fete was a triumph for Mhairi. She'd worked hard during the past few days, sewn everything required, and a bit extra. She'd pushed thoughts of Cuan aside whenever possible, and overall was feeling less broken hearted. She'd done what she'd set out to do, and now she had the fete to enjoy.

The sun shone brightly in a clear azure sky. All her parcels of quilt item orders had been picked up at the post office the previous day. She received orders via her website, and this provided a fairly regular income. So with the orders posted, everything else was available for sale at the fete. She'd worked well into the night preparing each item, and got up early in the morning to be ready for the fete.

She ate fresh fruit for breakfast — apple, peach and locally grown raspberries and brambles. Then she put on a cerulean blue cotton dress, stepped into her comfy sandals, and swept her hair back in a tidy ponytail. The dress was a tried and true favourite, washed so often the fabric had acquired a lovely softness and the blue had a vintage appearance.

Her complexion glowed from the effects of another day spent swimming in the sea, so minimal makeup was required — just a sweep of mascara and lipstick. No sea mist had prevented her from watching Cuan taking his daily dip, but whenever she'd seen him she'd looked away and focussed on her sewing. She was sure the slip stitching on the edges of her quilt backings were the most fastidious she'd ever sewn.

Stacks of quilts were folded on her work table along with quilted cushion covers and other crafted items. She loved quilting so much and put her heart into every one of them that it was difficult to sell her favourites. In an ideal world she'd have kept them, stacked them and piled them high to cherish and look back on. There were quilts she'd sewn in winter when snow fluttered outside her window in the city. No matter what theme those quilts had, to her they would always feel like winter, cosy and comforting. Each quilt captured a piece of time, an atmosphere of the season in which it was sewn. She was glad when a customer bought her quilts and sad when she had to parcel them up, seeing them for the last time, yet pleased they were going to someone else to cherish them. It was the double–edged sword that some other quilters, including her aunt and Hilda, understood.

There were pieces of fabric in her stash, some the size of a fat quarter, others just a scrap. She kept them until she was working on the perfect quilt to include them. Looking back at a finished quilt she'd recognise the vintage rose she'd stashed for over a year and now appliqued on to a floral quilt, or the butterfly fabric scrap sewn into a quilt block as part of a traditional quilt.

One day the blue dress she was wearing would be too worn to wear. She hadn't sewn a memory quilt yet, but she was going to, and when she did, a piece of her favourite cerulean dress would be part of it — reminding her of when she was a young woman, living in a cottage in Scotland by the sea one wonderful summer, trying to forget about a handsome chocolatier — and in that quilt, in the little scrap of dress fabric, she'd remember him forever.

Mhairi drank down a cup of tea to keep her going, and gathered everything she needed.

Her wall art quilts were wrapped and ready to be carried over to her stall. It wasn't far from the cottage and nothing was particularly heavy, just bulky.

Numerous stallholders were busy setting up and helping each other. There was a sense of anticipation, and everyone working together. The stalls had been set up the previous night with each one having a pretty canopy with scalloped edges in ice cream colours. Mhairi's canopy was strawberry and vanilla. It went well with the vintage rose and cream quilts she displayed. Vintage, coastal and floral were her main themes.

A few trips back and forth and Mhairi's stall was starting to look inviting.

The sun sparkled on the sea and the breeze was mild enough to ensure the air was pleasantly warm. It was still mid–morning, and there was every chance the day would be scorching hot. Speaking of which — there was Cuan further along the esplanade, wearing his white shirt sleeves rolled up to reveal those lithe arms of his, and a pair of classy trousers. He looked like money, and she supposed he was. Not that she cared. She did quite well for herself and her business had potential.

She'd received an email from a home decor company the previous day, but she'd been busy organising her things for the fete and intended dealing with them first thing on Monday morning. They wanted to acquire several of her new fabric designs to use on their products — cushions, table linen and tableware.

Her heart soared when she read the email. They'd seen her work via the other home accessory company who were incorporating her designs and were interested in offering her a deal. So the fete was part business and part celebration.

Cuan glanced over at her again.

Mhairi gave her ponytail a swish, and they both pretended not to see each other, but he'd obviously been watching her. She hated herself for feeling flattered.

'It's a gorgeous day for the fete,' said Hilda, displaying her quilted bags and purses on her stall next to Mhairi.

'It is, Hilda. I think we're going to be busy.' Mhairi looked out at the sea. Boats were arriving with islanders, some stallholders, others visitors hoping to enjoy the fun. The little harbour was bustling with activity and there was already a queue at a nearby ice cream stall. Weekend visitors alighted from a bus and headed straight to the pop–up open air cafe for something to eat and drink. The aroma of fresh baked cakes and scones wafted over to Mhairi. For the moment, she resisted treating herself to tea and a slice of cake as there was still lots to organise at her stall.

The postmaster and the grocer were armed with clipboards, walking around and ticking off the tasks completed. Mhairi and Hilda were tick–boxed, and Hilda vouched for Ione who had forgotten a bag of her fairy dolls and ran home to get it.

'Ione's got herself into a tizzy with the fete,' Hilda said to Mhairi. 'She's the excitable type.'

Mhairi looked at Ione's stall next to hers. Many items were still stuffed in bags or scattered around. She nodded at Hilda, and they both set about arranging the fairy dolls and cushions on the stall for her.

Mhairi noticed Big Sam keeping a lookout for Ione from his silversmith stall along at the jewellery section. She nudged Hilda. 'He's very protective of her.'

Hilda smiled. 'Another wedding for us all to go to soon I think.'

At that moment Hilda issued a warning to Mhairi. 'Don't look up, concentrate on this fairy doll I'm holding.'

'What's wrong?' Mhairi whispered.

'Cuan's staring over at you. Pretend you don't notice him so he'll go away.'

Mhairi and Hilda smiled and fussed with the little fairy doll, commenting on the intricate top–stitching on the dress. The doll's strawberry blonde plaits and pretty face reminded them of Ione.

'Has he gone yet?' Mhairi hissed.

'No, he's loitering,' said Hilda. 'Now he's talking to the postmaster and they're both nodding. Okay, he's walking away to his cottage.'

Mhairi was worried. 'You don't suppose he's wangled a stall off the postmaster?'

'No, Ethel said all the stalls were booked. There wasn't one left.'

Mhairi craned to search along the stalls. They were all taken. What was Cuan up to?

Cuan wished he'd been sharp enough to hire a stall. It would've been a great excuse to loiter near Mhairi.

Seeing her again without being able to talk to her was torturous. He hadn't seen her since she'd last shouted at him that they were done. Although it wasn't a pleasant memory, he'd gone over it a hundred times in his mind, wishing he'd said something, anything to convince her he wasn't the untrustworthy rat she suspected.

He went into his kitchen and set up a large tray with every truffle he had, even the ones with tiny rosettes fashioned with miniature leaves that took him ages to make from his special fondant. The rose fondants were one of his new recipes, but what the heck. . . he'd do anything for a chance to get close to her, and maybe explain that he wasn't a rotten swine. He'd overheard Ethel call him this in the post office when she was chatting to a couple of women, sewing bee ladies by the sounds of them. They'd been talking about how to sew a pleated skirt and ended up gossiping about how he'd upset Mhairi. 'He's a rotten swine,' Ethel said scathingly. None of them disagreed. Perhaps he was, unintentionally of course.

He opened his cooler where he'd created something truly special in the hope of giving these chocolates to Mhairi. A bunch of chocolate tea roses made from milk chocolate with fondant stems and wrapped in foil to resemble a bouquet.

He'd offered to give the postmaster a tray of truffles to be handed out in the refreshment marquee and to the stallholders. The postmaster was delighted.

Cuan wasn't being devious. His offer was genuine. It just happened to have the benefit of allowing him to approach Mhairi. If she accepted a truffle, then he'd run back and fetch the chocolate flowers. He didn't want to risk them melting in the sunshine as he wandered around with the truffles. But desperate times merited desperate measures, and so he intended using his chocolates as a sweetener. He wished things could be more straightforward. He wished he hadn't upset her over Vanessa.

Cuan headed out of the cottage, armed with the tray of truffles. He realised he wished a lot these days. Perhaps he should buy one of those fairy dolls Mhairi and Hilda were enthralled with, and make a wish with that? Nothing around here seemed too outlandish, not with a dressmaker who sewed magic and a black cat who disappeared in the blink of an eye.

But he'd been told that Thimble the cat liked him. This was a good sign apparently. Maybe he wasn't such a rotten, devious swine after all.

Ethel's two stalls were along from Hilda. An array of yarn, displayed by colour, was on the stall nearest. Her knitted shawls, scarves and wraps were on the other stall, and she wore a seashell pink shawl to advertise one of the intricate designs.

Next to Ethel was one of the sewing bee ladies with a crochet stall. She too had shawls, scarves and wraps, only hers were crocheted using Ethel's yarn. She'd gone for a jewel–coloured display with items ranging from emerald and amethyst to sapphire and ruby. The emerald shawl already had a sold sticker on it, but orders could be taken for this crocheted shawl in the same colour and design.

A sewing stall near Ione sold a selection of vintage style items including floral skirts and tops with sweetheart necklines. And down from there was Tiree's stall. Her beautiful dresses hung on rails.

Mhairi hurried back to her stall. 'I've bought one of Tiree's dresses,' she said to Hilda.

'Lucky you, which one?'

Mhairi pointed. 'The azure chiffon cocktail dress.' The beaded work on the hem and top sparkled in the sunlight. 'It reminds me of the sea. I don't know when I'll ever wear it, but I've snapped it up.'

'Oh it's lovely,' said Hilda. 'I love Tiree's dress designs.'

'There are so many beautiful things for sale.'

Hilda smiled. 'I've got my eye on a few things. We always end up spending some of our profits on a buying spree.'

Mhairi agreed. 'That's the fun of the fete.'

Ione arrived back with the bag of fairy dolls and thanked them for setting up her stall. She wore a pretty yellow dress with fairy applique pockets. 'I'll treat the two of you to an ice cream conc,' she promised.

'And I'll buy the lemonade,' said Mhairi.

All was fine for a little while. The fete was busy with people and the mood was cheerful. Then Ethel came running over to Mhairi with her shawl flapping behind her.

'I can't leave my stall for long,' she gasped. 'But just to warn you — Cuan's going around with a tray of chocolate truffles, handing them out for free. He's working his way down here.'

Mhairi panicked.

'Don't panic,' Ethel told her. 'We're your back–up. I'll knit his balls together for breakfast if he upsets you again.'

'That won't be necessary,' Cuan said, taking them unawares. He held his tray out to Ethel. 'Truffle?'

Ethel pulled her shawl tight around her shoulders. 'No thank you. You can stick your truffles up your trumpet.'

Cuan tried to smile.

Hilda pursed her lips and busied herself serving a customer who was interested in one of her new quilted sewing bags.

Ione, holding a fairy doll in either hand, leaned forward, looked at the tray of truffles and screwed up her nose. 'They look like wee jobbies.'

Mhairi stood clutching one of her quilts. She didn't know whether to run, cheer or laugh.

Cuan glared at Mhairi, as if it was her fault his ego had been pummelled.

He turned and stomped off.

Ethel put a reassuring arm around Mhairi. 'Are you okay, hen?'

'I am, Ethel. I just didn't expect him to come right up to me. I should've said something but. . . I don't react well when he's near me.'

Hilda stifled a giggle. 'I shouldn't laugh, but did you see his face?' She began laughing.

Ethel and Ione joined in the laughter, and soon all of them were giggling.

'I'll go and get our ice cream,' said Ione, still giggling. 'What flavour would you like, Mhairi?'

'Any flavour,' said Mhairi.

Hilda snorted. 'Except chocolate.'

Ethel guffawed and soon they were all laughing again.

Cuan heard the raucous laughter, handed the tray of truffles into the refreshment marquee, and went back to his cottage to rethink his plan to win Mhairi's affections.

One day he'd look back at the ridiculousness of the insults and laugh at them.

He looked around his kitchen and sighed heavily. The truffles didn't work. Maybe the bouquet of chocolate flowers would be better? Or perhaps he should walk right up to Mhairi, be bold and tell her he loved her, that he thought she still had feelings for him, and that they should clear the air of all the silly misunderstandings, upset and nonsense — and try again where they left off?

The latter choice was the most sensible, but he knew he couldn't do it. She wouldn't listen to him anyway, and Ethel was poised to knit a pattern with his unmentionables.

Armed with the chocolate flowers, Cuan ventured back out to the fete. He was very likely on a hiding to nothing, but he wasn't giving up on Mhairi without a fight.

Mhairi, Hilda and Ione had finished their ice cream and they'd been careful not to get any of it near their stalls. The heat from the sun had increased, and their ice cream had melted almost as fast as they'd eaten it.

Big Sam popped down to check that Ione was all right. He wore a kilt and a short–sleeve, tight–fitting top. He was a strapping lad, the tallest and strongest man at the fete.

'You've got quite a swagger in that kilt,' said Hilda.

He waggled his hips and made the fabric swirl. 'I like wearing a kilt, especially on days like this. I enjoy getting the air about my whistle.'

Ione smiled at him. 'You're such a rascal.'

He lifted her up, kissed her and placed her down gently. 'But you love me, don't you?'

'I do.'

He ran back to his stall leaving Ione watching him. 'He suits a kilt, doesn't he?'

'Will he be wearing one at your wedding?' Hilda asked her.

Ione blushed. 'That would be nice, wouldn't it?'

While serving customers, they chatted about men, marriage and what type of wedding dress Ione wanted.

'I want a fairytale wedding dress,' said Ione. 'Not with fairies on it obviously, but a fairytale style. We haven't set a date yet, but we will soon.'

'Don't look now, Mhairi,' Hilda said, 'but here comes Cuan again.'

'What's that he's carrying?' Ione shielded her eyes to get a better look.

Mhairi was tempted to peek, but Hilda reminded her not to look.

At that moment the postmaster made an announcement. 'Would everyone taking part in the annual shore race please make their way to the starting line.'

Cuan stopped. A race? He was a fast runner, always had been. He quickly scanned the competition. A few fit–looking young men were heading down on to the sand where a line was marked. The grocer was now armed with a starter's whistle as well as his clipboard.

Cuan hurried over to the postmaster. 'Can anyone take part in the race?'

'Yes, of course,' the postmaster told him. 'I didn't think you'd be up for it or I'd have invited you to participate. It's a hundred metre sprint along the sand.'

Cuan felt a rush of adrenalin. Mhairi was watching him, pretending she wasn't, but he saw the secret glances in his direction. If he could win the race, maybe it would break the tension between them. The atmosphere at the fete was one of participation. He'd been the outsider in the community, the grumpy one, and now the man who'd upset Mhairi. If he showed willingness to take part in their annual race, this would surely help with his reputation.

Cuan ran like blazes towards Mhairi, thrust the bunch of chocolate flowers into her reluctant grasp, then raced down on to the shore. The race hadn't started yet. The postmaster was walking towards the finishing line getting ready to cheer the winner.

'Good on you, Cuan, for taking part in the race.' The postmaster smiled and pointed over beside the grocer. 'You'll find a spare pair of flippers over there in the big cardboard box.'

Cuan scowled.

'Good luck. Hurry up now, the race is about to start.'

With visitors watching from the shore and the stallholders peering from the esplanade, Cuan felt obliged to put on a pair of ruddy flippers and stand at the starting line. He looked up at the esplanade and saw Mhairi watching him.

He cursed to himself and then thought. . . what the heck. Flippers or no flippers, he was going to try and win.

The grocer announced to the challengers, 'On your marks, get set. . . go!'

CHAPTER EIGHT

Chocolate Tea Roses

A cheer went up as the participants set off, flipper sprinting across the soft sand.

'Come on, Big Sam!' Ethel shouted, while Ione hid her face on Hilda's shoulder.

'I can't look,' said Ione. 'Is my Sam out in front?' She peeked, and saw that the kilted competitor was just behind Cuan who had a narrow lead on Jessie, Hilda's sister. Jessie was over from the islands for the fete. Jessie was a quilter and also known for her lovely cross stitch and embroidery patterns.

'Jessie's going for it,' said Hilda. 'Tying her flippers on with sewing elastic was a great idea.'

'And come on, Jessie,' Ethel yelled. 'She's giving the men are run for their money. I bet she does one of her infamous cartwheels if she wins.'

Hilda nodded proudly. Jessie might be approaching her retirement years, but her sense of adventure hadn't waned. She'd always been strong and sturdy. Years of crafting, quilting and working on her husband's fishing boat had kept her muscles mighty. Cartwheels were her party trick. She'd done cartwheels on the sand during a recent summer when the sewing bee girls had a wild night on the shore. The sand had been no problem, but whether the flippers would slow her down was another matter. However, Hilda had seen Jessie do cartwheels in her new novelty slippers at Christmas on a thick pile carpet, so maybe she would attempt one or two in the race.

Several competitors floundered and tumbled on the sand laughing. Horns tooted, music played and everyone seemed to be enjoying themselves — except Cuan.

Mhairi held her chocolate tea roses and stared in disbelief at the scene down on the shore. Fierce determination shone from Cuan's face. She'd never seen a man's legs move so quickly while he appeared to be getting nowhere fast. Her thighs ached at the effort he was putting into running, lifting his knees high so as not to trip. In flipper sprinting he was fast, even though the soft sand scuppered everyone's speed. But she supposed it made the race last longer and the hilarity was entertaining. It was only a fun event, one of several organised for the fete, though someone should've warned Cuan.

Ethel roared with laughter. 'Look at the shape of Cuan's legs. He looks like he doesn't know if he's coming or going. Those flippers are flapping like duck's paddles.'

'Is he beating my Sam?' asked Ione, still hiding into Hilda's shoulder.

'Only by a whisker,' Ethel told her. 'Or should I say, a flipper.'

The women laughed and cheered everyone on.

In all the excitement, Mhairi forgot she wasn't talking to Cuan and started cheering his name. 'Come on, Cuan, run!'

Was that Mhairi's voice cheering for him? He had to hope it was. Spurred on that his efforts had been worthwhile, Cuan raced for the finishing line. Never had one hundred metres ever seemed so long. But he was nearly there, nearly. . . when suddenly there was a thud behind him. Someone had taken a tumble. He dare not glance round in case he lost momentum. By the sounds of the swearing, Big Sam had come a cropper.

A roar of applause erupted from the crowd. Big Sam had face–planted into the sand and the back of his kilt had flipped up, exposing his posterior.

'Oh, would you look at that,' yelled Ethel. 'Big Sam's giving us a hairy–arsed smile.'

Hilda put her hand over Ione's eyes. 'Don't look. He's fine, but his bahookie is in full view.'

Ione forced herself to peek and then realised people were applauding her handsome kiltie. She started to jump up and down and clap excitedly.

'That's a lot of man to come home to, Ione,' a woman commented to her. 'No wonder you're always smiling.'

The race continued with a diminished number of runners. The majority had been scuppered, were knackered or couldn't do it for laughing.

Cuan kept going. Tail–end stragglers couldn't beat him now. Hearing Mhairi still shouting his name, he forced a spurt of speed that would've secured him the win if Jessie hadn't resorted to an unusual method for reaching the finishing line. Three cartwheels and she pipped him at the post.

The postmaster snapped a photo with his phone.

Loud cheers, applause and excitement sounded from the crowd of onlookers.

The postmaster walked towards Cuan who was bent over, hands on his aching thighs, catching his breath.

'Sorry, Cuan. Jessie just edged it. She's Hilda's sister.' The postmaster showed him the photo, enlarging the image on his phone. 'Her flipper is a smidgen over the line before yours. Although her other flipper is in the air due to the cartwheel finish, officially she gets the trophy.'

There was a trophy? Cuan nodded his agreement. 'Jessie deserves to win.'

'There's still the egg and spoon race later on.' The postmaster's pen was poised above his clipboard. 'Will I put your name down?'

Cuan shook his head. 'I've never been one for spooning.'

'How about the three–legged race?' the postmaster suggested. 'You'd need a partner for that, but I'm sure one of the local ladies would be happy to tie themselves to you.'

Cuan forced a smile. 'I'll think about it.'

The postmaster scribbled on his list. 'I'll pencil you in pending a partner.'

Cuan made his escape as Jessie was presented with her trophy.

He walked up to the esplanade towards Mhairi's stall.

'I must've looked a complete fool,' Cuan said to her.

Aurora overheard on her way to congratulate Jessie. She held up her phone to Cuan and smiled helpfully. 'I've got the whole race on my phone. I'll send you a copy.'

'Thanks,' he said, forcing a smile.

Aurora hurried away to join Hilda, Ethel and Jessie, and to take pictures of them for the magazine.

Cuan stood with Mhairi as the excitement whirled around them.

'Would watching the race make me feel better?' Cuan asked Mhairi.

She screwed up her nose.

'I'll keep it in my archives, filed under — only watch in cases of extreme emergency when you want to hear the woman you adore cheering on your stubborn stupidity.'

Her chocolate bouquet lay on her stall. 'I need to get these flowers out of the heat or they'll melt.'

'I could drop them off at your cottage. I assume the door isn't locked. Or I could put them in my kitchen and you could pop by later and pick them up.'

'The latter, but it might not be this evening. There's a party and dance after the fete and I'm going with Ethel and the other ladies.'

'A dance?' He gave her a sexy smile. 'Hopefully, you'll save one for me.'

She gave him a non–committal smile, but at least they were talking again. She handed him the chocolate flowers. He took them, smiled again, and headed over to his cottage.

'Was that you giving Cuan his chocolate bouquet back?' Ethel asked, hurrying back to attend to her stall.

'No, he's keeping them from melting,' Mhairi explained.

Hilda joined them. 'So have we all forgiven Cuan?'

'Sort of,' said Mhairi. 'He's trying to get back into my good books.'

Hilda grinned. 'Get into more than that by the lusty look he gave you.'

Mhairi blushed.

'Oh look, she's blushing again,' said Ethel. 'That's a good sign.'

'It's all the hot sun and excitement,' said Mhairi.

The women laughed.

Ione came over and joined them. 'Big Sam's put our names down as a couple competing in the three–legged race. I'm not sure I want to take part.'

'Och, it's just a wee bit of fun, Ione,' said Ethel.

Ione sighed. 'I know that, but the prize is a gorgeous sewing basket with loads of threads in colours that would be great for my fairies. I think I could win the race, but I'm worried Sam will slow me down.'

Ethel and the others tried not to laugh, especially as Ione was totally serious.

Mhairi offered some advice to Ione. 'Tell Big Sam he has to help you win this race.'

Hilda looked around. 'Where is he?'

'He's at his stall using his silversmith gadget to engrave Jessie's name on her wee trophy,' said Ione.

The postmaster approached Ione. 'You ran away before I could confirm your participation in the three–legged race.'

69

'I had to discuss my tactics with the girls,' Ione told him. 'But you can tick your box. We're definitely competing.'

'Great stuff.' The postmaster ticked the list and then said to Ethel, 'I don't suppose I could persuade you and me to have a wee go in the race?'

Ethel looked shocked. 'What? Tie our ankles together?'

The postmaster winked at Ethel. 'Wouldn't be the first time we've played kiss, chase and tie–up games when I caught you.'

Ethel sounded indignant. 'Nonsense, besides that was a long time ago when I was a silly lassie.'

The postmaster cocked his head at Ethel. 'Fond memories though, eh? Are you sure you don't want to join in the race?'

Hilda gave her a nudge of encouragement.

'Okay, I'll consider it, but we can't win. Ione needs to win the sewing basket.'

The postmaster didn't care about winning and scribbled their names on the list before Ethel changed her mind. 'I've put us down as competitors. I'll come and get you when it's time for the race.' He grinned. 'Unless you'd like to have a few practice runs just now.'

'Nope. I don't need to practice,' said Ethel. 'I've got a good memory.'

'We had some fun, didn't we, lass?'

'Away you go,' she told him, 'and attend to your clipboard duties. I've got my stall to deal with.'

Smiling, the postmaster walked away.

'Why didn't you ever marry him?' Ione asked Ethel.

'Because I married someone else. I wasn't actually brought up here. I moved here from Falkirk with my parents when I was a young woman and enjoyed a light flirtation with the postmaster. He was always cheery and never took anything serious, and I didn't think he'd take us serious, that I was a passing fancy.'

'Turns out he was serious about you after all,' Hilda added, knowing what had happened.

'Anyway, I first fell for a very handsome man who turned out to be a gadabout, then I had the flirtation with the postmaster, and not long afterwards I married a local lad who wasn't as handsome as the gadabout but was loyal and trustworthy.'

'Loyalty and trust matter more than looks,' said Mhairi.

The women agreed.

'But my husband was still a fine looking man and we were truly happy for many years until he passed. By then, I was past my prime and very settled in my ways in my cottage with my yarn and knitting. The thought of marrying another man didn't suit me.'

'And the postmaster has been chasing Ethel ever since,' Hilda concluded.

Ethel had a wistful look. 'Over the years I've had my moments with the postmaster.'

'We don't always end up with the man people think we will, do we?' said Hilda.

'This is so true,' Ione agreed. 'Look at me and Big Sam. No one thought we'd get together especially as I had a crush on Bredon the beemaster. He was lovely — all golden hair and gorgeous with a good nature, but I wasn't for him and it made me realise I preferred Big Sam with his strong muscles and kind heart.'

Mhairi wondered if she'd find this type of happiness, and whether Cuan was the man for her, or someone else she'd yet to meet? The deceitfulness of her past boyfriends had given her trust issues, but she'd been determined to get over them, to build her business and find someone trustworthy to settle down with. . . But there was no time to dwell on this as all their stalls became busy with customers.

Several people snapped up Mhairi's traditional design quilts. She had business cards with her website details and lots of people picked one up telling her they intended browsing her website and ordering online when they got home. They enjoyed seeing her quilt work, but when a particular quilt wasn't available, they were happy to order one to be made in the design they wanted. She also had a portfolio on her stall with pictures of the designs.

Judith bought one of her quilts. Mhairi offered her a discount.

'No, it's fine,' Judith told her. 'I'm buying this on behalf of the dressmaker.'

Mhairi was flattered. 'The dressmaker wants one of my quilts?'

'She does. She saw your website and likes your designs, particularly those with elements of the sea. She'll love this.'

Hilda sold most of her bags and other little quilted items, and when Mhairi glanced over at Tiree's dress rack it was empty.

Ione's fairy dolls attracted a lot of attention and her stock seemed to have diminished substantially.

Ethel's yarn and knitting was extremely popular, and Mhairi bought a selection bag with twenty small balls of yarn in different colours from Ethel's new range to use for a crochet project.

The home baking stalls were continually busy. Mhairi loved cherry cake and bought a slab of this along with a bag of soda scones — and a jar of the beemaster's honey.

'Lunches are being served to the stallholders in one of the marquees,' said Judith. 'I'd be happy to mind any of your stalls while you grab a bite to eat.'

'I'll take you up on your offer, Judith,' said Ione. 'My tummy's rumbling with all the excitement. My price list is on the stall.'

Judith stood in for Ione who ran along to get Big Sam to have lunch with her. One of the jewellery sellers kept an eye on his stall for him.

Ione relayed Mhairi's advice as they headed over to the marquee. 'You have to help me win the race this afternoon. You just have to. The sewing basket prize has vintage threads and some of them have a sparkle effect. I want them for my fairies.'

He put his arm around her and gave her a reassuring squeeze. 'I'll try to win for you, Ione.'

She gazed up at him. 'Great. Now let's go and get lunch and make a plan of action.'

The marquee was jumping with people but Big Sam cleared a way through and secured them a table for two. He joined the queue for tea, sandwiches and cake and brought a tray over with two mugs of strong, milky tea, fairy cakes with sprinkles and her favourite tomato sandwiches. He cut the crusts off the sandwiches and ate them. Ione didn't like crusts.

A string of important business calls had trapped Cuan in his cottage, but the day was still young. He had plenty of time to cajole Mhairi to dance with him.

The postmaster had also phoned to ask if he had a chocolate cake to spare for the lunches. Someone had unintentionally sold their milk chocolate gateau at one of the baking stalls and they needed one as it was advertised on their menu.

Cuan put a large chocolate cake in a box and hurried over with it to the marquee. He was making his way through the crowd when he passed by Big Sam and Ione sitting at a table having lunch. Sam was eating a sandwich crust and using a teaspoon to scoop something out of Ione's mug of tea.

'Quite a race we had, eh, Cuan?' said Big Sam. 'But the best woman won.'

'She did indeed.' He frowned, wondering what was wrong with Ione's tea.

'It was poured from a height and in a hurry, causing a bit of bubbling around the rim,' Big Sam explained. 'I'm scooping the wee bubbles out. Ione doesn't like bubbles in her tea. They remind her of soapy water.'

Ione smiled sweetly at Cuan, all prior insults totally forgotten.

'Are you going to start dating Mhairi?' Ione asked Cuan.

'That's my plan,' he said.

Big Sam flattened the last bubble in Ione's tea, put the spoon down and looked thoughtful at Cuan. 'Would you like a bit of friendly advice?'

'About what?'

'Handling women, especially that sneaky Vanessa.'

Cuan's brows rose in surprise.

'Yes, I know all the gossip.' Big Sam had seen her coming out of Cuan's cottage the day she'd kissed the chocolatier.

'Go on,' Cuan encouraged him.

'Well. . . I think you should keep that woman out of your life, and definitely keep her from coming between you and Mhairi, which is what she wants. I've met women like her before and they're pure poison. They pretend they want you, when they really don't, but they don't want other women to have you, so they inveigle themselves into your life like poison ivy, tightening their hold until they squeeze the good out of everything.'

Cuan listened, interested in what Sam had to say.

'I'm a man who likes women, but Vanessa gives me the heebie–jeebies,' said Big Sam. He squeezed Ione's hand. 'Though I only love one woman.' Then he looked at Cuan. 'So take heed, don't let Vanessa near you or your cottage again. If you have to deal with her for business, do so, but only when other managers are involved.'

Cuan nodded. 'I intend to keep her away from here and only meet with her in the city when necessary. I won't be inviting her here.'

Big Sam frowned. 'But she's already here. I saw her at Tavion's flower stall as we were heading to the marquee. Even sniffing his fresh cut roses, she looked like she had a smell under her snooty nose.'

Cuan gasped. 'Vanessa's here?'

'Yes, so watch your tail,' Big Sam warned him. 'She's a viper.'

Cuan's mind whirred in panic. 'What was she wearing so I can pick her out quickly from the crowd before she finds Mhairi.'

'A woman's business suit, tight skirt, jacket lapels sharp as blades. High heels. And her jewellery. . .' he shook his head. 'Fashionable crystal bracelet and necklace that look like they'd rip into you. They wouldn't, but that's the impression.'

'What colour is her suit?'

Big Sam studied the colours in his kilt and spotted a similar shade on the edging. He lifted up the front of his kilt to show Cuan the colour. 'This shade of teal blue.'

Ione gasped, as did a couple of others sitting having lunch nearby.

Big Sam smoothed his hem down again. He held his hands up and said loudly, 'Sorry folks, a wee slip of the kilt.'

Cuan dumped the chocolate cake down on their table and ran from the marquee to search for the viper in the teal blue suit.

CHAPTER NINE

Sewing Bee Fashion

Vanessa prowled around one of the sewing stalls, picking up the pretty hand–sewn garments between two fingers and then discarding them as if they were soiled dishrags.

The stallholder was one of the ladies from the sewing bee and wondered who the snooty woman was. On a hot summer day when everyone else was casually dressed for the fete, she looked like she belonged in a meeting in the city instead of circling around the stalls. Clearly, she disapproved of everything, including some of the sewing bee ladies' fashions, so why was she here? Suspicious of her motives, the stallholder signalled to Ethel who alerted Hilda who nudged Mhairi. The look on Mhairi's face showed she knew who it was.

'It's Vanessa,' said Mhairi. This was relayed back up the chain of ladies until several stallholders had her in their sights.

By now Vanessa was looking at the bric–a–brac stall with sheer disdain.

Ethel hurried over to Mhairi and Hilda.

'Run down on to the shore before Vanessa sees you,' Ethel urged Mhairi.

Mhairi sounded angry. 'I'm not running away from her.'

'You're not running away,' Ethel clarified. 'You're outsmarting her. Obviously she's not at the fete to enjoy the home baking or hand–sewn bargains. She's here looking for you.'

'Or Cuan,' said Mhairi.

Ethel shook her head. 'No, she's wanting a confrontation with you. Trust me, I know her type.'

Hilda and Ione agreed.

'Hurry up,' Hilda urged her. 'We'll cause a distraction so she won't see you running down to the shore.'

'Vanessa won't follow you on to the sand in her high heels,' Ethel added.

Hilda sounded anxious. 'She's getting nearer. She's at the embroidery stall. She'll see you.'

Signals were being relayed between the sewing bee ladies and even the postmaster had been alerted. Several of them swooped in on Vanessa to give Mhairi time to decide what to do.

'Would you like a lucky dip to win an embroidery kit?' one of them asked Vanessa, blocking her view.

'No, I don't embroider,' Vanessa snapped.

'How about a raffle ticket to win a cuddly toy?'

Vanessa ignored her.

'What about the tombola? Have you given that a go?'

Vanessa walked on not giving a reply.

The postmaster stepped into the fray. 'Hello, there. Lovely day we're having. Will I put your name down for the egg and spoon race?' He checked his watch. 'It's about to start in a few minutes.'

Vanessa scowled at him. 'Are you kidding me?'

'No, it's about to start soon.'

Vanessa eyed him up and down. Was he really that stupid? 'I'm not here for any silly races.'

The postmaster looked at her. 'Well, you're here at our fete. I don't see you having bought anything. You didn't even glance at the home baking. You're not interested in our lucky dips or raffles. So, as one of the organisers of this event, I have to ask myself — what is this lady doing here at the fete when she's not interested in any of it?'

'I have a right to be here just like anyone else,' she snarled at him.

The postmaster, used to dealing with disgruntled people queuing with their parcels and not getting their stamps to stick, didn't flinch. 'And I have a right to be suspicious.'

Ethel walked past. 'You're wasting your time, Vanessa. You should leave before you cause a rumpus.' She continued walking.

Hearing her name, Vanessa reacted, taken aback by the woman wearing a shawl and now walking away from her.

The postmaster joined Ethel, leaving Vanessa momentarily floundering, and a lot less sure of herself. She suddenly felt she was being watched. She looked round and there was a black cat sitting on the shore wall staring at her. She blinked and the cat had gone.

Mhairi stood amid the egg and spoon crowd on the shore, her face shaded by the wide brim of a sunhat. She watched Vanessa look around, searching for her. She loitered at Mhairi's stall.

And then she saw Cuan making a beeline for Vanessa. He hurried through the crowd. The esplanade was filled with people viewing the stalls, ambling along eating ice cream and enjoying the relaxed atmosphere. The only tension emanated from Vanessa and the clash that was about to happen with Cuan.

Mhairi panicked. What should she do?

She waved frantically at Cuan, hoping he'd see her down on the sand, but he was focussed solely on reaching her stall.

She took her hat off and waved it wildly. Come on, Cuan, look at the shore, she urged him.

Still Cuan continued, and then. . . he heard a loud, 'Meow.'

He looked round and there was Thimble, green eyes wide, staring at him. He paused. The cat jumped off the shore wall down on to the sand. Or so he thought. When he looked over, the cat had gone. But then he noticed Mhairi waving at him, beckoning him urgently to her.

Without hesitation, Cuan jumped over the wall and landed on the sand. He ran over to her.

Mhairi saw that Vanessa was none the wiser about what had happened. She was still hanging around the stall, searching the crowd, convinced Mhairi would be back at her stall soon. Hilda kept an eye on it for her. Vanessa ignored Hilda, which suited Hilda just fine. She knew where Mhairi was, and now Cuan was with her.

'Vanessa's here. I didn't invite her,' Cuan insisted.

Mhairi nodded at him. 'I believe you. Ethel and the others suggested I come down here to avoid her.'

'I came to warn you as soon as I heard. I was in the marquee. Big Sam told me he'd seen her.'

'I have no problem confronting her, but I don't want any of her troublemaking to taint the fete. Everyone is having a great time.'

'You did the right thing coming down here out of her way,' he assured her.

He looked so handsome, she thought. If Vanessa hadn't turned up, everything could have worked out fine.

'Don't let Vanessa spoil things.' He stepped close to her. 'I do still have to work with her because of the deal.'

'I'm not asking you to forgo the deal.'

'I couldn't even if I wanted to now because I've signed the contract. I'm obliged to make it work. Vanessa is the one who initiated the deal and I'm not in a position to renegotiate.'

'I understand.'

He held her hands and pulled her close. 'I wish I could solve this issue with Vanessa, but it's complicated.' He paused and let her hands go. He gazed out at the sea. 'I seem to wish a lot of things these days.'

'Me too,' she said wistfully.

'Such as?' he asked her.

'I'd love to live in a cottage here instead of going back to the city. The more time I spend here, especially on days like this, the more I long to find a way to make it happen. A practical way, not some daydream.'

He wanted to tell her she could live with him, but he knew the timing was completely wrong. He'd have to wait until they'd had a little more time together without the shadow of Vanessa lurking in the background. He thought he'd handled Vanessa quite well during recent meetings at the hotel in the city. He'd given her no personal encouragement about getting involved with her outwith business. Now here she was stepping into his private life. Big Sam was right, he thought. Vanessa was a troublemaker.

'Hurry up you two,' the grocer said to them, thrusting spoons and eggs into their hands and more or less pushing them towards the starting line. 'The egg and spoon race is about to start.'

'I think we're being egged on,' Cuan joked.

Mhairi laughed, and they quickly lined up with the other participants.

'Eggs on your spoons,' the grocer announced. 'Get ready, and. . . go!'

And they were off. Mhairi and Cuan were near the centre of the race.

Eggs were being dropped all around them, amid raucous laughter.

Cuan tried to go as fast as he could without dropping his. 'I haven't done this since I was at school.'

'Neither have I,' said Mhairi.

They were among the front runners as they approached the finishing line. Cuan put on a spurt of speed but his egg wobbled and despite trying to rebalance it, the egg toppled off his spoon. Mhairi hurried on and finished fourth. Not bad, she thought, and she hadn't dropped the egg once.

The postmaster congratulated the winner and runners up.

'That was a wee shame, Mhairi,' said the postmaster. 'I thought you were going to take third place.'

'It was good fun,' she told him. She wasn't disappointed at all.

'And it's not your winning day, Cuan,' said the postmaster. 'Beaten again by a woman.'

Cuan smiled at Mhairi. 'Oh I think I won after all.'

The postmaster smiled at them. They made a fine couple.

Vanessa was displeased with the selection of sandals for sale at one of the stalls. But they would have to do. She couldn't walk on the sand in her high heels. She'd seen Cuan and Mhairi in the race. They looked ridiculous. But now she knew where they were.

Vanessa grabbed a pair of sandals that were the least tasteless, and went to try them on for size.

The stallholder stopped her. 'No, you can't try them on with bare feet.'

Vanessa frowned at her.

'Hygiene,' the stallholder emphasised. 'You'll need to wear a pair of socks to try them on.'

Vanessa sighed. 'All right, I'll buy a pair of socks.'

The selection was less to her taste than the sandals were.

The stallholder helped her narrow down the selection. 'I have lovely sparkly owl socks, or these ones with kittens or butterflies.'

Vanessa glared at her impatiently. If looks could kill. 'Give me any socks. I don't care.'

Unperturbed, the stallholder said, 'You could buy three pairs. I have a special offer on for the fete — three pairs for the price of two.'

Vanessa's nostrils flared. 'Just give me a pair of socks! Any socks.' Then she glanced at a pair that no way she'd ever want. 'Except those ones with the ferrets on them.'

'They're foxes.'

'Whatever.'

The stallholder gave Vanessa a pair of sparkly owl socks.

Vanessa put them on and then tried the sandals on for size. To her surprise, the socks and sandals were very comfortable. 'I'll buy these.' She thrust her heels at the stallholder. 'Put these in a bag for me.'

Vanessa dumped her shoes in her car and then ventured to the shore.

Ethel came running as fast as she could on the sand up to Mhairi and Cuan.

'Vanessa's heading this way. She's wearing sandals and sparkly owl socks.'

Cuan blinked in disbelief. 'Owl socks?'

Ethel sounded serious. 'It doesn't bode well. It shows the level of deviousness and determination a diva like her is prepared to resort to. She's ditched her fancy heels so she can walk on the sand.'

'But why the owl socks?' asked Cuan.

'It's what was available. She said she didn't care. She wouldn't walk on the sand with her bare feet apparently, so she's kitted herself out with socks and sandals.'

'Maybe Vanessa has a fun side to her?' Mhairi suggested.

Ethel shook her head. 'No, she was snippy to the stallholder and insulted her fox print socks insinuating they were ferrets.'

'Would couples taking part in the three–legged race please proceed to the starting line,' the grocer announced.

'Sorry, I have to run and tie myself to the postmaster.' Ethel ran off leaving Mhairi and Cuan smiling at the situation.

'Is it always this crazy here during the summer?' Cuan asked Mhairi.

'Only since you moved here to live at your cottage. When I've visited my aunt during the summer holidays, it was always very relaxing.'

Cuan grinned at her. 'I see they're offering sailing trips from the harbour along the bay. Maybe we should jump onboard and leave Vanessa floundering on the shore.'

'No, she'd put on a pair of flippers and swim after us. That shark wouldn't give up easily.'

'We could go and hideout in my cottage,' he suggested.

'What? And miss out on all this fun?'

He smiled warmly. 'We are having fun, aren't we?'

'Ask me later, when Vanessa has gone.'

A tall, handsome local lad approached Vanessa. He wore jeans and a short–sleeve, clean white shirt that showed off his toned arms. 'Hi, fancy joining me in the three–legged race? I'm looking for a partner, but all the best women are taken — except you.'

She sounded irritated. 'No, I'm not interested.' She'd lost Mhairi and Cuan in the crowd. Where had they gone? So many people were on the beach taking part in the races or watching family and friends participate.

He wasn't easily discouraged. 'Are you sure I can't entice you? You're a fit–looking woman. I'm a fast–runner. We could win this. Come on, let's have a go.'

'Do I look like I want to take part in a stupid three–legged race?' she snapped at him.

He smiled and looked down at her socks. 'You're wearing owl socks that sparkle in the sunlight.'

'Go. Away.'

He shrugged his broad shoulders and walked off casually.

Mhairi and Cuan had been encouraged by Ethel and the postmaster to take part in the three–legged race.

'Everyone line up for the race,' announced one of the organisers. The grocer was waiting at the finishing line, standing in for the postmaster.

'Remember, we're not running to win,' Mhairi reminded Cuan as he tied them together. She'd explained about Ione wanting the sewing basket. He was happy to be taking part.

Beside them, ankles tied together, stood Ethel and the postmaster. He was grinning and had his arm firmly around Ethel's waist. Hilda was manning their stalls and waved down to them. They waved back.

'Big Sam looks determined to win,' Cuan whispered to Mhairi.

Mhairi nodded and smiled hopefully.

Vanessa saw Mhairi and Cuan lining up. She beckoned urgently to the local lad.

'I've changed my mind. I'll do it.'

He smiled, delighted, and hurried to tie them together. 'What's your name?'

'Vanessa.'

'Let's win this, Vanessa.'

'I don't care if we win or not, I just want to beat those two.' She pointed at Mhairi and Cuan.

'No problem,' he assured her. 'As I said, I'm a fast runner. Hold on to me and I'll steer you straight.'

'Look who is taking part in the race,' Ethel said to Mhairi and Cuan. She motioned to a couple further along the starting line.

'Why is Vanessa running in the race?' said Cuan. 'And why is she partnered with one of the builders who is working on my cottage extension?'

Before any of them could figure out Vanessa's motives, the organiser signalled the start of the race.

Mhairi and Cuan got off to a fast start. She had her arm around him and could feel the taut muscles in his torso. Their strides were even, well matched. Cuan forged ahead, mindful that they had to let Ione and Big Sam win.

No one was quite sure of Big Sam's technique and whether it was entirely within the rules, but as this was just a fun event at the fete, there was no chance of them being disqualified. He'd tied Ione's ankle to his, as normal, but he appeared to be carrying her with one strong arm around her slender body with a grip of steel. Although her tied leg moved like a piston with his, her feet barely touched the sand.

Vanessa had started to get a feel for the speedy rhythm of her partner. He was a fast runner, very fast, but somehow she managed to keep up. This secretly excited her. She hadn't experienced this type of giddy happiness in a long time.

'Come on, Vanessa,' he urged her. 'Run your heart out.'

And she did. They were now among the front runners along with Big Sam and Cuan. Closing the gap behind them was Ethel and the postmaster. All thought of how they weren't as fast as they used to be was cast to the wind. The sand slowed many couples down but didn't have this effect on Ethel and the postmaster.

No couples dropped out, but many faltered, getting fankled as they tried to keep in step with each other. They'd slow down or pause, losing their momentum. As with previous events, there was plenty of laughter and cheers.

Mhairi glanced at Vanessa as they were now neck and neck with each other. Vanessa was laughing. What a weird and wonderful day this was, thought Mhairi, determined not to be beaten by her.

Mhairi felt a surge of pace from Cuan and forced herself to run even faster.

Big Sam and Ione were ahead of everyone and set to win. And they did. The grocer snapped their photo but it was clear to everyone watching that they were the winners.

Second place was being fought for by Mhairi and Cuan against Vanessa and her partner. As the two couples crossed the line, Mhairi hoped they'd just edged it. The grocer gave her the thumbs up confirming they had.

Ethel and the postmaster ran hard and came in fourth. Both of them were delighted. The postmaster kissed and hugged her. She made no attempt to stop him.

Vanessa didn't like losing, while her partner thought third place was okay.

'There was tough competition,' he said. 'But you ran well. We're not used to each other. If we'd practised we might have won, though I think Big Sam had it nailed.' He smiled at her. 'Fancy partnering up with me again? Want to go with me to the fete dance?'

'There's a dance?' She didn't know this. She thought the fete ended around tea time.

'A party and a dance in the marquees.'

She looked around. Mhairi and Cuan had given her the slip again, merging into the crowd.

'Will everyone be at the dance?' she asked.

'Yes, it's the highlight of the fete. You'd enjoy it.'

'I don't have a dress.'

'There's nothing wrong with the clothes you're wearing.'

'It's a business suit.'

'Dresses are for sale at some of the stalls.'

She thought about the owl socks and unflattering sandals. But of course she had her heels in the car.

'Any decent dresses?'

'I'm no expert on fashion, but there seemed to be plenty of pretty dresses.'

'Okay, I'll see you later at the dance.'

'It's a date,' he said, smiling as she walked away from him.

Not with me, she thought. She had another date in mind.

At a dress stall Vanessa rummaged through the selection of cocktail length dresses in her size. 'Some of these are quite acceptable.'

The stallholder paid no heed to her uppity attitude. 'Is it a dress for the dance you're looking for?'

'Yes.' She held up a little navy blue cocktail–length dress embellished with sequins.

'Going with a handsome man?'

'Sort of.'

'What's his name?'

She realised she didn't know. He'd told her but she hadn't cared to listen.

Vanessa searched for a label on the dress she was thinking of buying. 'Did you make this?'

'Yes, the sequins are sewn on to the hemline by hand. I'm part of the sewing bee. We share patterns and techniques.'

In a makeshift changing room Vanessa slipped out of her suit and into the dress. 'It fits. I'll take it.'

CHAPTER TEN

Rose Garden Romance

Mhairi wore the dress she'd bought from Tiree to the fete dance. She'd draped a silk scarf in shades of blue around her shoulders. As she walked from her cottage to the marquee, a warm evening breeze wafted through her azure chiffon cocktail dress and the beading on the hem and top sparkled like the sun glistening on the sea.

The fete stalls were empty but music, laughter and chatter filtered from the two marquees — one specifically for lively dancing and the other for the party buffet and plenty of fun. The marquees were decorated with fairy lights and bunting and were already busy with people enjoying themselves as Mhairi approached them. She'd agreed to meet Cuan there after clearing up her stall and going back to her cottage to freshen up and change into her party dress. She wore her hair down and was looking forward to the dancing which was in full flow by the sounds of the upbeat music and activity.

Mhairi stepped inside and saw Cuan waiting for her. He waved and hurried over.

'You look beautiful.'

He looked handsome in his cream shirt and dark trousers.

A live band played a reel and people were whirring around the dance floor. She saw Ethel and the postmaster and Ione with Big Sam. He wasn't the only one wearing a kilt. A few men wore kilts. Although the dance wasn't specifically a ceilidh, there were plenty of Scottish reels to be enjoyed along with a good old–fashioned knees–up. Mhairi loved the traditional music and dancing.

The inside of the marquee was draped with twinkle lights and bunting. Two bars were set up to provide a constant flow of refreshments, and if anyone wanted something to eat and a sit down to catch their breath from the hectic dancing, there was the party in the other marquee.

Most of the women, including Mhairi, wore flat shoes to participate in the energetic dancing.

'Come on, let's join in.' Cuan pulled her into the fast–moving reel.

For the next few songs they danced their hearts out, and it felt great to let go of all the recent tension and upset and lose themselves in the happy atmosphere.

Taking a break, Cuan asked Mhairi if she'd like a drink from the bar.

'I soft drink, something with lots of ice.'

She stood to the side, watching Big Sam dance with Ione and Judith. He had one on either arm, swinging them both around. She wasn't sure who screamed louder with glee, Ione or Judith? Probably Judith who hadn't come with a dance partner, but at events like this no one needed to. There was always someone to dance with, and many of the reels were full participation with whole groups of friends linking arms or holding hands as they circle danced for joy.

The sewing bee ladies had agreed to attend the dance together, but that plan had been cast to the wind as the wild partying and merriment took over. Aurora filmed some of it, but kept being pulled into the jigging.

Cuan came back with their drinks. He'd opted for the same as Mhairi, a tall glass of iced lemonade. He tipped his glass against hers. 'To you and me.'

She smiled at him. 'Cheers.' She sipped her drink and felt it refresh her senses. She had no idea where she'd found the energy to last the entire day at the fete amid being hunted by Vanessa and running in two races. She hoped Aurora had captured it all on film and wanted a copy. Perfect viewing for a rainy day when she was back in her flat and needing perked up. She never imagined she'd run in a three–legged race with Cuan especially against Vanessa and the builder. And then she wondered. . . where was Vanessa?

Ethel and other sewing bee ladies had heard she was going to the dance. Rather than be annoyed, Mhairi thought a confrontation would set Vanessa straight about thinking she could just turn up whenever she wanted and cause friction. Mhairi didn't want to spend the summer looking over her shoulder, concerned that Vanessa was in the vicinity.

Mhairi scanned the faces, searching for Vanessa — and there she was, entering the marquee wearing the dress she'd bought and her high heels.

'Vanessa's arrived,' Mhairi whispered urgently to Cuan.

'Stick close to me,' he said in a reassuring tone. 'We're not going to let her spoil our evening.'

Mhairi nodded. They were going to have to deal with her at some point.

Vanessa hadn't seen them yet, but she was looking for them. She might have seen them sooner if the builder hadn't bounded over to her blocking her view. He gave her a hug and kissed her cheek. Vanessa floundered, unprepared for any sort of affection. He'd caught her off guard.

'You look smashing in that dress, Vanessa.' He smiled at her. This was the first time she'd noticed the dimples in his cheeks and what a cute smile he had. But she still wasn't fussed about his name or what he did. A farmer or fisherman probably. It was of no interest to her.

'Would you like a drink?' he offered.

'I'll have a Manhattan cocktail.'

The dimples in his cheeks deepened as he smiled. 'Okay.' And off he went to the bar.

'Will you excuse me for a few minutes?' Cuan said to Mhairi. 'I want to ask my builder what Vanessa is up to.'

'Great idea.' Mhairi stood where she was, sipping her lemonade while Cuan hurried over to the bar. A group of revellers were up dancing and separated Mhairi and Vanessa, blocking them from seeing each other.

Cuan and the builder talked at the bar, confiding their concerns about Vanessa.

'I understand your situation, Cuan. I know she's a difficult woman, but when I first saw her on the shore, I liked her face and asked her to join me in the race. I could tell by her attitude she doesn't belong here. But I was curious to know — what happened to this woman, she's broken, but is she beyond repair? Then I caught a glimpse of her, the woman she could've been, laughing and running beside me in the race. When it finished she disappeared again, and the cold–hearted side of her was back. So I asked her to go with me to the dance.'

'You feel sorry for her?'

'I suppose I do. I thought to myself, what if I had Vanessa here with me, could I mend what's broken? Vanessa would be one hell of a challenge, but to tell you the truth, I don't think I'll get the chance.

She'll leave here tonight and may never come back.' He shrugged. 'Just a feeling in my bones.'

'Has she asked about me or the building work on my cottage?'

'No. She doesn't even know my name, never mind what I do for a living. I'm her invisible date for this evening. The strange thing is, I'm the only man here tonight who has really seen her and wants to get to know her.'

Cuan nodded. He was a good–hearted soul.

A barman placed the builder's order on the counter. 'One lemonade shandy and one Manhattan cocktail — with a cherry.' He winked.

'Good man.' He picked up the drinks. 'Talk to you later, Cuan.'

Mhairi listened to Cuan explain the situation while watching Vanessa sipping her cocktail on the far side of the marquee.

'Come on you two,' the postmaster beckoned to Mhairi and Cuan. 'We're going to do a reel.'

Mhairi and Cuan joined in with the numerous people taking part. The music was fast and lively, and it was only when they stopped she noticed Vanessa heading straight for them.

'Here she comes,' Mhairi warned Cuan.

Big Sam and Ione were nearby. Ione was still excited about winning the sewing basket. The atmosphere around them was happy until Vanessa approached.

'I know you've been avoiding me, Cuan,' she said, totally ignoring Mhairi. 'So can I remind you that we are working together on the new product design.'

'This is the weekend. It's the local fete. Was it necessary to come here? I have a meeting early next week at the hotel.'

'I brought the new chocolate box. It arrived after you left the last meeting. I thought you'd be keen to see it. I've got it in the car if you'd like to take a look. We could discuss it in your cottage. It's rather noisy in here don't you think?'

'No, bring it in. I'll drop it off at my cottage and discuss the details at our next meeting.'

Vanessa stomped off. Her car was parked further along the esplanade. Several minutes later she marched in with it. 'Here, do whatever you want.'

Cuan took the package. 'I'll discuss this next week.'

Vanessa stared at Cuan and became argumentative. 'You don't really believe you belong in a place like this?' She glanced around, giving disapproving looks at the people around them, including Ethel, Hilda and Ione.

'I certainly do. This is my home now.'

'You belong in the city. This is just a stupid phase, Cuan.' She glared at Mhairi. 'And so is she.'

Before Mhairi or Cuan could speak up, Big Sam stepped forward and his voice sounded loud in the marquee as there was a brief lull in the music.

Big Sam looked at her. 'What is wrong with you, Vanessa? You're a lovely looking, intelligent woman with a good career. You'd be better spending as much time making yourself happy as you do making other folk miserable.'

Vanessa hesitated. His words made her unsure what to say. If it had been Cuan or Mhairi who'd argued with her, she was ready for them. But confronted by Big Sam with everyone around looking at her jarred her confidence. Without saying anything, Vanessa walked out of the marquee.

No one tried to stop her. They'd all had enough of her attitude.

The builder stood at the entrance watching her get into her car. He heard the engine sputter and conk out.

He went over to give her a hand.

'Pop the bonnet open,' he said to her through the window.

She released the catch, and he pushed the bonnet up. She sat in silence.

He made a few adjustments, and then closed the bonnet.

'Try to start the car again,' he called to her.

She turned the key in the ignition and the engine roared into life.

She glanced at him, and for the first time since he'd met her, he noticed that she looked upset. She didn't even manage to thank him for his help.

He watched her drive off into the night.

'Goodbye, Vanessa,' he said quietly, and then went back to the dance party.

Mhairi enjoyed dancing with Cuan. Everyone had a great time and round about midnight, when the revellers were starting to make their way home, she draped her silk scarf around her shoulders and walked with Cuan to his cottage to pick up her chocolate bouquet.

The scent of the roses and other flowers in his garden wafted in the warm night air.

He opened the door, which he'd left unlocked, and led the way inside through to the kitchen.

'If the summerhouse had been up we could've sat outside,' he said.

She peered out the window at the dismantled summerhouse. 'You will have the builders reconstruct it, won't you?'

'Yes.' He leaned close to her and pointed. 'It's going to be over there, along with the rose bushes.'

'I'm glad. We hardly had a chance to enjoy it.'

'We'll have time again,' he assured her.

For some reason, she felt extremely sad, perhaps because time was the problem. It would be July before the construction work was finished and then there was the garden to sort, and Cuan would surely be busy reorganising his kitchen and extension. She sensed their time would wisp away, and before she knew it, she'd be getting ready to leave and it would be August.

'What's wrong, Mhairi? You look anxious.'

She forced a smile. 'Just thinking. . .'

'About leaving?'

She shook the anxious feelings off. 'It's still June. I'm here until August. I don't want to ruin my time here worrying about having to go back to the city.'

'We'll still see each other, won't we?'

'I hope so.'

He pulled her close and held her tight.

They both looked out at the garden.

'What else would you like in the garden?' he asked.

'Me?'

'Yes, if this was your cottage, if you lived here, what would you want?'

'More flowers along the borders. Night scented flowers so I could enjoy the fragrance in the evenings. And another rose tree over there.' She paused, hearing the enthusiasm in her voice.

'Don't stop.'

She shrugged. 'I'm getting carried away with things. This is your house, not mine.'

He wanted to tell her that it could be her house too, but he couldn't risk making a mistake again and pushing their relationship too fast.

'I welcome your suggestions,' he said.

'Have you looked at the new chocolate box design?'

'No, I dropped it off and then ran back to the dance.'

The package was lying on the kitchen table. He opened it. His name was printed bigger and bolder.

They smiled at each other, and then she told him the news about the email she'd received.

'I'm going to contact them on Monday morning and accept their offer.'

'Your designs are lovely. I'm delighted for you. I'm sure they'll look great on the linen and tableware.'

She wandered over to admire one of his cakes.

'Are you busy on Monday afternoon? I'm baking a new type of chocolate cake. I'd welcome your opinion on the taste and texture,' he said.

'I am busy. Judith told me this evening that the dressmaker has invited me to her house for afternoon tea. I don't know why she's invited me. She doesn't invite many people, so I'm flattered and intrigued.'

'Did Judith give a hint about what the dressmaker wants to chat to you about?'

'No, I've no idea.'

He smiled. 'You can give me your opinion on my new cake another time.'

'I'd love to, but I'm no expert.'

'You don't need to be. You just have to use your senses to assess the taste and texture.'

'My senses?'

'Yes, can I show you?'

She nodded.

Cuan set up samples from two chocolate cakes, one milk, one white chocolate, along with a selection of truffles.

'Do you trust me?'

She frowned. 'Yes, of course.'

'Can I borrow your scarf?'

As she nodded he gently pulled the silk scarf from around her shoulders.

She started to giggle. 'What are you up to?'

He folded the scarf to make a silken blindfold. 'Close your eyes.'

She was still giggling as he tied the scarf on her as a blindfold and positioned her closer to the table with the selection of cake and truffles.

'What do you want me to do, Cuan?'

'Taste the chocolate using deeper senses.'

'How do I do that?'

He placed a morsel of cake to her lips. She opened her mouth and accepted it. Her taste buds tingled with the delicious mix of chocolate and fresh cream. The cake sponge was light, the buttercream icing sweet and smooth, and the fresh cream rich and cool.

'Don't think about the chocolate or the cake — think deeper, how does it make you feel?'

She hesitated, slightly embarrassed, and yet. . . wanting to tell him.

She blushed.

'You're blushing.'

'I know.'

He didn't push her any further. 'I'll take the blindfold off.'

'No. I want to try this. Let me try a little more.'

He lifted a piece of dark chocolate truffle filled with strawberry mousse topped with a pink rose fondant, and put it up to her lips. 'What do you think of the flavours?'

She tasted it. 'It's dark chocolate, I can taste the hint of sweet bitterness, and there's strawberry. The strawberry scent is mixed with something else. Fragrance of roses?'

'If you were to describe the feelings involved, what would they be?'

She thought for a moment and then said, 'Romantic and yet passionate.'

He leaned down and kissed her gently. She kissed him back, and for several moments she felt afire, wrapped in Cuan's loving embrace.

He finally untied the silk scarf and draped it around her shoulders.

She blinked, still blushing, and eager to kiss him again, but mindful of getting intimately involved.

'I'd better go,' she said softly.

He smiled in agreement. 'I'll walk you home.'

Cuan carried the chocolate bouquet. He kissed her goodnight when they arrived at her cottage. 'I had a great day and evening with you. I'll speak to you tomorrow.'

She kissed him, gave him a hug, accepted the bouquet and waved him off.

Judith arrived in her car to pick Mhairi up for afternoon tea with the dressmaker.

'It's not far,' said Judith, 'just a wee bit difficult to find amid all the trees in the forest above the coast. We'll be there in a few minutes. And I love you in that tea dress. The dressmaker will be delighted to see you wearing it.'

Mhairi smiled. She'd decided to wear the beautiful vintage rose and cream tea dress the dressmaker had given her. The wraparound style made it a perfect fit.

They headed away from the shore up towards the forest. Sunlight shone through the trees and they drove with the windows open in the hot afternoon sun. Trees arched above the narrow roads and created a sense of heading into a secret realm.

'Here we are,' Judith said, parking in front of a traditional, two–storey cottage. It had a vintage ambience, as if it belonged to another era. The garden was lush with flowers and greenery.

Mhairi followed Judith into the living room with its pale blue–grey walls and shelves packed with rolls of fabric. The dressmaker sat at a table with her laptop open beside one of her sewing machines. She wore an elegant crepe de chine dress a few shades darker than the walls. She smiled when she saw Mhairi.

She was very pretty, of retirement age, with her blonde hair pinned up in a chignon, and beautiful blue eyes that gave Mhairi the impression she could see right through her.

'Lovely to meet you, Mhairi. I was looking at the quilts on your website. I like your designs, especially those with a sea theme. I loved the quilt Judith bought from your stall at the fete. It's ideal for my living room.' She pointed to where it was draped over the back of a sofa.

'I'm pleased you like my work, and thank you for inviting me here this afternoon.'

'My pleasure. I thought we could have tea outside in the garden. It's such a lovely summery day.'

'I'll set it up,' said Judith, and scurried through to the kitchen. She'd prepared the sandwiches and cakes before driving down to pick up Mhairi. All she had to do was make the tea. The cups, saucers and silver teaspoons were set on a tea tray. She carried it through to the patio table while the kettle boiled.

The dressmaker invited Mhairi to sit beside her so she could indicate the quilts she liked on the website.

'This art quilt design is of particular interest to me. The way you've incorporated the layers of different fabrics gives the impression of a sea storm. You've captured the atmosphere — from the stormy grey sky to the sea foam. It's exquisite. Do you still have this quilt and is it for sale?'

'Yes, it's one of my favourites.'

The dressmaker gave her a knowing look, as if she understood how difficult it was to part with a cherished quilt.

'Will you sell it to me? I'd like to frame it and hang it on that wall over there.'

'I'd be happy to sell it to you.' She'd kept it wrapped, protected from harm, but it would be far better for it to be seen and enjoyed.

'Excellent. Judith will arrange the payment.' She closed the laptop. 'Thank you for wearing the tea dress. It suits you.'

'I love the vintage print fabric,' said Mhairi.

'That's another thing I wanted to talk to you about, so it's handy you wore the dress. See the different hues in the rose print and the way the green leaves merge so well with the cream background?'

Mhairi looked at the fabric of her dress — really looked. 'Yes.'

'Could you design a quilt like that?'

'Yes, I think I could.'

'I'll commission you to make it for me. Judith will sort out the payment.'

Judith pushed a silver trolley through the lounge and out to the patio. It was laden with dainty cut sandwiches, chocolate gateau and cherry cake.

'Shall we?' The dressmaker headed outside. Mhairi walked beside her while Judith poured the tea.

94

They sat around the patio table.

'Help yourself, Mhairi,' said Judith.

Mhairi selected a couple of cheese and salad sandwiches and a piece of cherry cake. 'I love cherry cake.'

Thimble wandered over from relaxing in the shade under the flowers. He settled down nearby.

Judith chose a slice of chocolate cake. 'I wonder if the chocolatier would approve of this gateau?'

'Cuan McVey has started to settle in now. I heard he ran in one of the races in the hope of impressing you, Mhairi.'

Mhairi felt a blush start to rise in her cheeks. She sipped her tea.

The dressmaker smiled. 'We're making her blush, Judith. She must really love him.'

Mhairi blushed profusely.

'Don't concern yourself with Vanessa,' the dressmaker assured her.

The tone of her voice and the look she gave Mhairi was extraordinary. As if the dressmaker knew something.

Mhairi faltered. 'I eh. . . Cuan and I aren't going to let her affect us.'

The dressmaker smiled again, and then they all enjoyed their afternoon tea and chatted about sewing and fabrics galore.

Cuan ran up to Mhairi's cottage. The door was open and Mhairi was busy working on her quilts.

Cuan hurried in. 'I was going to phone you, but I wanted to tell you the news in person.'

'What news?'

'Vanessa has quit her marketing job with the hotel and gone to London to work for another company.'

Mhairi's hopes soared. 'Is this true?'

'Yes. The hotel management phoned me.'

Mhairi did an impromptu jig in the lounge. Cuan joined her. Amid their laughter and cheers, Cuan elaborated with a few more snippets. 'Apparently her trip to the fete, and especially what Big Sam said to her, made Vanessa rethink her values. She'd been wanting to work in London for a while, but never really went after a new job until now.'

'That's perfect. You can still have your contract, but not have to deal with Vanessa.'

'And Vanessa gets a job she really wants.'

They had a cup of tea to celebrate.

A few weeks later, the building work was complete on the chocolatier's cottage and the extension was everything Cuan had wanted.

The garden looked lovely, especially with the summerhouse rebuilt, adorned with roses, and an extra rose tree and night scented flowers.

It was July — a hot summer evening. The scent of the sea mingled with the flowers.

Mhairi was outside in the summerhouse. 'Do you want me to help you?' she called to Cuan.

He was busy in the kitchen. 'No, relax, you're being spoiled.'

Mhairi sat in a comfy chair watching Cuan serving up the dinner he'd promised to cook for her. The summerhouse was aglow with fairy lights and a pretty tea candle lamp on the table.

Cuan carried out a tray with two plates of his special chocolate truffle pasta.

'This is totally delicious,' said Mhairi.

It would be August soon, but it didn't matter. She wasn't going back to the city. She was staying with Cuan in his chocolatier's cottage by the sea. When her aunt came home, she'd enjoy the best of both worlds, living with Cuan and spending time working with her aunt at her quilting and crafting cottage.

Cuan smiled and had a mischievous glint in his eyes. She was sure he was up to something, but he denied it and told her to relax and enjoy their dinner.

He'd promised her he'd take things slowly, but he'd bought her a ring — diamonds set in rose gold, a modern vintage design he hoped she'd love. He'd asked Ethel and the other ladies for their input, secretly finding out what type of engagement ring Mhairi dreamed of having. Big Sam helped him design it. Her ring finger was the same size as Ione so he knew it would be a perfect fit.

Mhairi had planned to put relationships and romance on ice and enjoy a wonderful warm summer sewing her quilts and relaxing by the sea, but things didn't turn out the way she'd planned. And she was glad. She'd met Cuan, the man she would marry — her handsome chocolatier.

End

Now that you've read the story, you can try your hand at colouring in the illustrations.

De-ann has been writing, sewing, knitting, quilting, gardening and creating art and designs since she was a little girl. Writing, dressmaking, knitting, quilting, embroidery, gardening, baking cakes and art and design have always been part of her world.

About the Author:

Follow De-ann on Instagram @deann.black

De-ann Black is a bestselling author, scriptwriter and former newspaper journalist. She has over 80 books published. Romance, crime thrillers, espionage novels, action adventure. And children's books (non-fiction rocket science books and children's fiction). She became an Amazon All-Star author in 2014 and 2015.

She previously worked as a full-time newspaper journalist for several years. She had her own weekly columns in the press. This included being a motoring correspondent where she got to test drive cars every week for the press for three years.

Before being asked to work for the press, De-ann worked in magazine editorial writing everything from fashion features to social news. She was the marketing editor of a glossy magazine. She is also a professional artist and illustrator. Fabric design, dressmaking, sewing, knitting and fashion are part of her work.

Additionally, De-ann has always been interested in fitness, and was a fitness and bodybuilding champion, 100 metre runner and mountaineer. As a former N.A.B.B.A. Miss Scotland, she had a weekly fitness show on the radio that ran for over three years.

De-ann trained in Shukokai karate, boxing, kickboxing, Dayan Qigong and Jiu Jitsu. She is currently based in Scotland.

Her colouring books and embroidery design books are available in paperback. These include Floral Nature Embroidery Designs and Scottish Garden Embroidery Designs.

Also by De-ann Black (Romance, Action/Thrillers & Children's books). See her Amazon Author page or website for further details about her books, screenplays, illustrations, art and fabric designs. www.De-annBlack.com

Romance books:

Sewing, Crafts & Quilting series:
1. The Sewing Bee
2. The Sewing Shop

Quilting Bee & Tea Shop series:
1. The Quilting Bee
2. The Tea Shop by the Sea

Heather Park: Regency Romance

Snow Bells Haven series:
1. Snow Bells Christmas
2. Snow Bells Wedding

Summer Sewing Bee
Christmas Cake Chateau

Cottages, Cakes & Crafts series:
1. The Flower Hunter's Cottage
2. The Sewing Bee by the Sea
3. The Beemaster's Cottage
4. The Chocolatier's Cottage
5. The Bookshop by the Seaside
6. The Dressmaker's Cottage

Sewing, Knitting & Baking series:
1. The Tea Shop
2. The Sewing Bee & Afternoon Tea
3. The Christmas Knitting Bee
4. Champagne Chic Lemonade Money
5. The Vintage Sewing & Knitting Bee

The Tea Shop & Tearoom series:
1. The Christmas Tea Shop & Bakery
2. The Christmas Chocolatier
3. The Chocolate Cake Shop in New York at Christmas
4. The Bakery by the Seaside
5. Shed in the City

Tea Dress Shop series:
1. The Tea Dress Shop At Christmas
2. The Fairytale Tea Dress Shop In Edinburgh
3. The Vintage Tea Dress Shop In Summer

Christmas Romance series:
1. Christmas Romance in Paris.
2. Christmas Romance in Scotland.

Romance, Humour, Mischief series:
1. Oops! I'm the Paparazzi
2. Oops! I'm A Hollywood Agent
3. Oops! I'm A Secret Agent
4. Oops! I'm Up To Mischief

The Bitch-Proof Suit series:
1. The Bitch-Proof Suit
2. The Bitch-Proof Romance
3. The Bitch-Proof Bride

The Cure For Love
Dublin Girl
Why Are All The Good Guys Total Monsters?
I'm Holding Out For A Vampire Boyfriend

Action/Thriller books:
Love Him Forever
Someone Worse
Electric Shadows
The Strife Of Riley
Shadows Of Murder
Cast a Dark Shadow

Children's books:
Faeriefied
Secondhand Spooks
Poison-Wynd
Wormhole Wynd
Science Fashion
School For Aliens

Colouring books:
Flower Nature
Summer Garden
Spring Garden
Autumn Garden
Sea Dream
Festive Christmas
Christmas Garden
Christmas Theme
Flower Bee
Wild Garden
Faerie Garden Spring
Flower Hunter
Stargazer Space
Bee Garden
Scottish Garden Seasons

Embroidery Design books:
Floral Nature Embroidery Designs
Scottish Garden Embroidery Designs

Printed in Great Britain
by Amazon